PICK ONE AT RANDOM

MARION CRICK

Chapters

Pick one at random

By Marion Crick
Published by CCLLP

Copyright 2019 M Crick

This book contains adult content from the start.
Please do not continue if you would find this offensive.

ISBN 978-0-9928281-6-5

February 2019

This is a fictional story.

Some of the names, titles, sequencing, areas and dates in this book have been amended to ensure that this work portrays a fictional experience, rather than those of any other individuals, companies or circumstances.

Any similarity is purely coincidental. This book is also an expression of the personal opinion of the author.

Acknowledgements

Marion Crick would like to thank her family, friends and past and present acquaintances for their help and support in creating the tapestry that is her life and the source of many of the tales within this text. Without this rich variance of situations that they have provided, her work would not be as diverse as it is.

Thank you for the experiences of the good, the bad, the difficult, the love, loving, companionship and wealth of observations you have all provided in your own ways.

Also to the people Marion never met, just observed from a distance. They have added colourful and valuable fabric to the mix that has been woven together.

Inspired by the song featuring Horace Wimp.

Ode to romance

Writing of love can be as difficult as finding love.
It flits all ways, with delight, being cruel, emotions erupt,
It lands, and it leaves, hovers, flutters like a dove.
The realisation can be slow, evolve, or
thunderbolt abrupt.

The souls involved each have a different approach,
The path of true love is not a set route.
Different types can find love together, without reproach,
But some fall apart, their paths in dispute.

Love is not about sex, lustful advances or carnal desire,
It's far more complicated than that, as our
lovers discover.
Search your world for those you know, attract
and admire,
Your answer may not be obvious, but a result
to uncover.

Lovedon
The first book by Marion Crick
ISBN 978-0-9573125-4-8
Original July 2013/ Second Edition February 2019

Chapter 1
Singledom

'Tell me her name! Just tell me her name!', she screamed at Sam as tears rolled down her cheeks, reddened with sheer disbelief.

'HIS name is Rupert!', he hesitated, adding 'and we're moving in together!'.

'So you're leaving me for him! Seriously? Rupert! Seriously?'.

For a second, his recent change and now clear deceit all made sense. Then the thoughts, hopes and memories in her mind piled on top of each other as the line of her very being toppled like dominos and did not stop. Sam, her now ex long-term boyfriend, tried in vain to console her over the coming days as he cleared his things from their flat and moved to his new love nest with Rupert in West London. Mel stayed over with her parents the final night he moved out. 'Just locked up and I will post you my key. Sorry! X', was his parting text and she sobbed uncontrollably that night.

Mel's days became weeks became months and her life took no form that she was proud of. She forgave, she drank, she wallowed, she sobbed, however she also pulled through and the thought of starting again could now be glimpsed.

She knew that she was a bit 'vanilla' as a person, hopefully with a few sprinkles of excitement and intrigue, but still vanilla. Pleasant, enjoyable, but not the first-choice pick for 'team life'. Mel knew she was energetic, vivacious, and everything had gone sort of as planned. She had met a great fun guy, Sam, they had had a great time, moved in together, spent the best years of her life so far setting herself on course for happy ever after. He realised he was gay, she got dumped and she mourned for too long, years in fact, and now found herself in the completely updated world of dating. Wow! How that's changed, and although intriguing, it's difficult. 'Cattle to market' she thought when she first detailed her profile as she entered the 'dating pond', also wondering what pond life would appear.

Who was she now? She knew who she was in her twenties, but life, Sam, mortgages, management, alcohol had all blended into her now single life, and she just didn't want that. She has so much to give, to share, to love...just who with?

Loneliness? For sure, but it was deeper than that.

Mel's Profile

> Melissa here. Call me Mel! Refocusing my life on my future, I hope with a good, soon to be companion. Busy work life with little social balance, but fun and outgoing. A South London lady looking for friendship, fun, and to share.

Melissa...Mel for short

Melissa was born in Orpington, south of London, and her parents still lived in this well to do, leafy suburb. She despised the name Melissa, given to her in memory of some distant late aunt, who was a bit of a dragon by all accounts. Melissa means 'Bee' in Greek, and apparently her late aunt was always a 'busy bee', according to her parents. They liked this thought and applied it to their youngest with great pride. The arrival of Mel on TV's *Neighbours* in the summer of 1987 was her opportunity to shorten her name, and everyone took to the change, even though she was Melissa, and Mel on TV was Melanie. 'Hey, who cares!' was her response to any unwanted questioning, although her parents refused to accept this change, even to this day. The arrival of the Spice Girls in 1991 reignited the name debate, but she carried on, and they all soon forgot.

With two lively sisters to contend with in her formative years, and being the youngest, she had learned quickly how to be feisty in conversational combat. She enjoyed it, but knew this could appear dominating. Mel curtailed this where she needed to, but this was not very often. The three daughters were sometimes referred to as the 'spice' girls with changed names, the eldest being 'Pretty Posh' spice, the middle being 'Sporty' spice and Mel being a cross between Baby and Ginger spice, and just as gobby. For those she allowed close to her, she found it was of more detriment than good. She was in medium shape, quite unremarkable really, and the recent lack of exercise had seen some unwelcome curves appearing. Melissa had tried to keep fit, which Sam had enjoyed when they were together, but managerial desk work at a PR company in recent times and the new muffin-top were on her list to go, or at least reduce! Pilates classes had helped keep her slight frame supple and she was thankful for her diligence in this regard. The belly button piercing had looked provocatively sublime some 15 years ago, complementing her flat stomach contours. Sam's arousal had been heightened subsequently in their love making, he sometimes fixated as he energetically entered Mel from above, but clearly not enough to stop him from searching for something more, something different. WTF had she done to deserve singledom?

She had thrown herself into work post separation, she knew no other option, and her exercise routine had dwindled as her employer identified her new attention to her work and, 'sympathetically' was only too willing to fill the time void that had been created by her break up as her newly evolving world unfolded. Sam had also had his uses when it came to her arachnophobia in dispensing of any large unwelcome spiders in the bathroom. He had been replaced with a large, strategically placed long handled loofah to 'dispose' of any unwelcome eight long-legged creatures making their home in her flat.

Mel still thought of herself as a 'young 46', and now as a singleton, the world was hers to enjoy. Her long-term, often argumentative relationship with Sam had ended some years back and had left her on her own, although Sam and Rupert had been together ever since. Sam had been ten years older than Melissa and seemed always to be anxiously looking to conquer the life that was his, to find the key to his world. Well now he had! The nature of the split was sudden and unexpected, noting that she had happily felt she had discovered herself when she met him. It had been a whirlwind of fun, sex sometimes verging on a little weird, holidays, intimacy and passion, all now gone, but not forgotten.

She had once loved her rather bohemian style growing up. She still missed it. It always suited her style she thought, with soft hazel eyes and flowing locks. Age had been a cruel mistress and she still in part resented Sam for stealing these years from her. Her eyesight had suffered in her mid-thirties and the decision to have her eyes lasered was prompted by the suggestion of upping her glasses prescription to ever thicker lenses. 'Sunglasses only from now on!' she insisted at the time, although this had not always been possible. She had a fair complexion, with brown straight hair that headed to auburn, which she regularly challenged with a hair colour heading darker, also helping to cover a few grey hairs that were spreading, much to her repeated annoyance. Her straight hair had originally been worn long, happier days as she remembered, and the length had shortened as the years ticked by. If she retired tomorrow, she would grow it back out again, she promised herself, slumping slightly at the fact that both retirement and her follicular ambitions were many years away.

The South London flat was small, plain, neat and tidy. Magnolia walls, with the odd splash of colour in the curtains, blended with mood lighting and large black and white framed photos. Mel had been prudent with her money at the right time and squeezed herself, with help from the bank of Mum and Dad, to buy a two-bed flat in a red brick 70's built block. They had willingly funded the same for all their girls and did not flinch when it was her time to buy. It had been a financial struggle, taking on a lodger at one point to pay the bills, before Sam had swept her off her feet and moved in, much to the annoyance of the lodger who soon left due to the incessant groans coming from the bedroom at all hours. The second bedroom had been for guests, storage, as a 'dog-house' when she and Sam had argued, which accelerated towards the end. The arguing increased and became a blur, but she recollected that he became an almost permanent resident of this box-room before the split.

Mortgaged of course, she had owned her flat, and determinedly held on to it, and the days following her separation had been a blur, with much soul searching as to what had happened. Over time, she had forgiven Sam for leaving, and he had blossomed since his new relationship had begun, but she still grieved the loss left in her life. She kept in contact with Sam, and as their relationship had reached a new friendship level, also strangely with Rupert. Sam still clearly cared for her, but he had been true to his inner being and she admired his conviction. The print pages that provided hollow advice on how to get back on your feet were recycled and the blur turned into a fog of weeks, which led to a winter of months, four long years or so had elapsed before she felt that she could look for a companion again. She was not sure if she was ready, and acutely aware that the dating game had changed so radically since she was last involved that she questioned if she was more uncomfortable about the protocol than the person she had agreed to meet. She knew she could be a bit uptight and this might not help.

Her managerial role now provided enough for her to keep the flat without the financial support of others, although she knew her ageing parents would help out if she asked, which she point blank refused to do. The spare room was the one place in the flat which always held busy memories for her. Like Piccadilly Circus at times, her social life with Sam had been hectic, and the room always had a guest or Sam in the room at some point. His lover, Rupert, had stayed a few times and latterly she often wondered if the 'guest' and Sam had been in the same room. She carefully painted the walls to change it completely, to help erase, to forget what had gone before. 'Cheating bastard' ran through her mind as the tufted roller ran over the walls with fresh paint, satisfying for just a moment before the reality of what she was trying to achieve reverted to the forefront of her thoughts.

'Wine o'clock' she thought and headed to the fridge.

Sam

Mel was everything to me in the first few years. I was smitten by her from the day we met at a conference in Doncaster. The location was not romantic, but an alcohol-fuelled evening had led to future days and nights of passion and adventure.

I had soon loved her, her family, her everything, it all seemed so natural, but somehow I could not commit. As time ticked by, this really bugged me. I could not understand that this loving utopia I found myself in just did not do it for me. The pressure to maybe marry, maybe start a family, maybe commit pushed me further away. I got angry, and I know I took this out on Mel. The arguing, the shouting was not her fault, just me being a prat. But then, one day, I found myself accepting that I had always been curious about men. It was like scales falling from my eyes, and all became clear. As I became more curious, I found myself understanding Grindr, but I think I nearly got caught by Mel, so switched to my phone. She didn't say anything! As it happens, there was no need, with Rupert at his office one day hooking up with me and not letting go. Rupert was now everything to me.

I had tried really hard not to cheat on Mel, I really had, but it just happened, after work and my mind body and heart were lost to her. I didn't know where I was to be honest, but the door to physical love for her was gone. Lust for Rupert drenched my mind and we made love as often as we could, hiding this both from Mel and from colleagues until the truth would out. Wow! That was a difficult week. I still love Mel, I think I always will, but more as a sister, than the great love and lover she once was to me.

Sunday Lunch

Since the separation, Sundays had been the hardest day of the week to avoid loneliness, especially the middle of the day. Mel knew the end of the day would naturally see anxieties rise as she focused on the working week ahead, and the mornings could sometimes be a blur from a binge of alcohol the night before, social calendar allowing. But how to fill the middle? Sure, the family had rallied round when Sam left. Lunch with Mum and Dad, or her sisters, or all, or at her flat had been welcomed. However, as everyone began to be confident that Mel would survive, the attention had fallen away and she often found herself wandering into London to stimulate her mind with a museum or gallery view. She had even gone to lunch in recent years with Sam and Rupert. It had been fun, but still somewhat depressed her. Netflix, radio and books had become good friends, but solitary in their style, with the occasional trip to the cinema alone, which she had somehow found a bit creepy. Mel would often listen to a radio play on the sofa whilst neatly filing, cleaning and painting her nails. Indeed, she had become quite the expert at her manicure skills, a treat to herself, and these were often admired by many of her colleagues in the office.

Melissa wanted to be true to herself, but her current life was not true to her, or her dreams, or her needs. Her desire to have a family of her own had once been a powerful motivator in her life, only to be extinguished by the departure of her long term partner and her body clock now ticking loudly. This was of great sadness to her, and to her parents, grandparents in waiting. Initially, their sex life had been fantastic, however Sam's physical desires had become more obscure as their time progressed and he had become darker, even aggressive, in mood when the topic had come up. Latterly, Sam had never shown great interest in sex, box room used or otherwise, and eventually it became clear his needs were being met elsewhere. She had once found a listing for Grindr in the home PC browser history. Surprised, she had not thought to ask why, but now starkly understood.

The thought of walking a dusky beach on a holiday alone, paying premium rates, with no mates made her shudder. She wanted to be loved, to be hugged, to share, to be held, to feel safe, secure, desired and to desire. She did not want to die alone!

Fantasy dreaming? Perhaps, but still possible.

Chapter 2
Mum never told me...

Greg

Mum never explained what love was about, well not to me anyway. Well, I don't think she did and I was not listening if she had. Or was it that I just couldn't filter or fathom the information? Can't compute, my mind's computer says no!

Dad had engineered our early days to establish order in the kids, well boys anyway! And now, as an engineer, nothing had changed, although my model car collection had got a lot bigger, polished regularly of course, my dream vehicles only obtainable in 1/12th scale. 'Everything in order' rang in my ears from my memory bank of my Dad's voice placing pressure on me and my older brother to be neat, tidy, correct. Gregory, my name, means 'watchful' or 'alert' in Greek, and as a youngster this had inspired me to be just that! Watchful, purposeful, but as it transpires a keen under-performer in the 'alert' description, usually taking no actions after being watchful. And when it came to relationships, to a great extent I was a bystander in taking action in securing love and companionship.

My father's orders had become my lifestyle, almost natural order, the only problem being is that that world was gone, and now I float in the ocean of the new world, alone and sometimes feeling 'sans' life preserver. Bollocks, what a mess! The irony is that everything I do, the way I live is somehow controlled, even restrained in precise order, but my life is far from ordered in the way I want it.

It's like I've got nerd, geek or bore tattooed on my ever more apparent forehead, and if that doesn't do it, making the big assumption that I can secure a date, not having messed it up already in initial communications online, I only have to have a stilted conversation with a lady and she 'swipes left' and my profile is deleted. So will my life be at this rate!

Spontaneity, natural wit, cheeky, interesting, debonair, cute, sharp dresser, wealthy...would not be found on Greg's profile, as you can see.

Greg's profile

> Heading towards the big Hawaii (5-0) and still single. The sort of man who was always asked to see a girl home because everyone knew she would be safe, and she was. Excitement tends to be for someone else, but still a good man looking for a good lady to share life interests. Surrey based engineer.

Greg, nerd in short

Greg was a typical average boy, loved by his family, comforted and tortured simultaneously by the boredom of blue collar and middle management life, estranged in relationships, and generally getting along ok, albeit alone.

The infant grew into a boy child, to a relatively unconfused and respectable adolescent too...well that's really where it starts to stop. Did he ever really grow up? Sure, he had physical needs and changes that were covered over, but did he mature? In all things, well no!

The importance of pushing forward with his career post education was always instilled in him by generations of his family as a priority. This was somewhat overbearing, but he was comfortable and his family supportive, so that's what he did. It was his life, they just forgot to tell him that part! Greg started work almost as soon as his washing was folded by his Mum on his return from Plymouth University and applied his understanding and education, learned on the job, and meandered slowly up the ranks of the small business. The inherited west-country twang he had acquired on his course soon left him as he worked on the outskirts of West London. The daily drive to and fro was not as challenging as he had first envisaged, as long as he left early, music and radio filling the car.

Sure, the trappings of daily working were exactly that, trappings, as he grew older. A modest home, later to be inherited with a shared and not so stretching mortgage, a sporty, spotless silver version of an average car, and the odd European holiday with friends. Many would welcome such a peaceful and unassuming life, but it was not a life shared. Indeed, it was quite the opposite from that he had known and cherished as a boy, in the bosom of the family unit, mother, father, brother, sister. It all seemed so natural, so easy way back then. The reality now of finding a partner seemed poles apart from his memories of more complete days.

'Mundane!' was the fullest description that Greg could come up with for his engineering work. The initial challenges of learning had all been overcome and getting through the day was now usually the biggest challenge. To some extent, he liked it that way. His work was neither interesting, nor uninteresting, just an endless workload that needed to be filtered to reach the company's project aims. Deadlines arrived, were met, and were completed. He met his tasks, ticked a box, went home. However, this daily un-fulfilment was another burden he bore. Both ends of his life, personal and work, could not continue to be unfulfilled. He would go mad, or worse. Something had to give, surely…please!

And for Greg, this is where the personal 'rub' lay. The weeks of life had turned into months, years and then decades. The big birthdays of 30 and 40 beckoned the potential of a new dawn in his mind, that new contacts would lead to love, to commitment, to sharing, even passion. Ironically, as the years had ebbed by, his lustful desires had subsided, mostly anyway, but the urge for companionship had grown ever stronger. Trying to be cool had faded to being chilled in his heart. But the demands of rigours of life, of work, had played a different hand, as they do for hundreds of thousands of people as he realised and took some consolation from, and as the horizon of 50 years old appeared in his diary. Far from being exciting, the cloud of being alone became somehow darker. This was never in the script entitled 'The story of Greg'.

His circle of friends had lessened in the last decade. Some had coupled up and started new directions, families and the like. Others had simply become more insular in their outlook as costs rose, and salaries didn't and the social spend to be spared became unaffordable. Others fairly became comfortable in their own skin and the need to share time and experiences with others simply dropped off their agenda. Greg had largely ignored this gradual social slide for some years, but became lonelier as the years ticked by. Social media had disguised this in part. He had been an early adopter of some sites, with many contacts and friends, but he understood after a while that it seemed the more he connected, the less he knew anyone.

Like many, as he had got older, he had become more set in his ways, his routines, complacency was a visitor, and with no others to love, or love him, why should he bother changing? His routine life choices began to reflect this, from his car, his cheap but correct cropped haircut, to his attire, to his overall outlook and none of them were helping his chances of finding the one thing he really wanted, which was to share what remained of his life with a trusted, loved friend.

Greg's mother had given him a copy of *Men are from Mars, Women are from Venus*, as a type of 'don't give up' present one Christmas. He was embarrassed and quickly tucked it away under the obligatory M&S socks, tie, pants and assorted unimaginative toiletries that were the norm at the festive season. He dipped in and out of the text during dry January, which at least had the benefit of passing the time, rather than providing any helpful pointers. He had taken relationships for granted as something that would happen…and that was where it started to unravel.

Sure, he had had a few relationships, which he had enjoyed, but the gaps between each grew longer, as the lengths of involvements became shorter. What did he have to do to catch a break?

Obsession, frustration, even depression?

He was no longer obsessed with finding a partner, although he had spent many hours, if not days in the past doing so. Sure, it was frustrating, but this desire had somewhat expired into resignation, as he had rather given up hope of ever finding real companionship. He had found it troubling as he approached his 40th birthday some nine years back. He only had to look on dating sites to know that he was not alone to be consoled for a nanosecond, before still knowing he was alone. Many had commented that he seemed to be out of sorts and distracted, as confusion swirled around his mind as to why he was alone. This 49th arrived. A big birthday for him, the last before being 50, and was a flag in the sand to him with the hope of starting his next decade with someone. So far, t was not to be and this hung heavily with him in his heart. He took a trip away for the big day, telling his family that he had a great day arranged with friends. They were pleased, however, he had not, and drove to the south coast to have fish and chips and a long walk along the empty drizzle spattered beach to think about where he really was. It was not the first time he had taken himself off to a destination just to be alone, but it was more poignant on this day.

It was autumn, his favourite time of the year, with the summer heat now dissipating, shadows getting longer, the leaves turning and falling, and the morning mists sometimes with a faint smell of stale bonfire smoke as he undertook his daily morning drive. This time he felt that he may be reaching his personal autumn, not having had a summer of life beforehand. His eyes welled for a moment, a sensation he rarely experienced.

Greg's reflections were deep and endless, even empty at one point. He reached no firm conclusion to his desires for his future, but felt better in taking time to reflect on what could have been, and what still might happen. He did however resolve not to be so concerned about the issue. 'What will be will be!' He exhaled as the last chip was consumed from the paper wrapper, before bundling up the wrappings and throwing them in the bin. His drive home seemed more uplifting than the darker trip down to the seaside and he was thankful that to some extent this big 49th birthday had been better than many for his own long-term wellbeing. Winters were darker for him, but somehow comforting in their way, and he made the best of any social opportunities that might arrive over Halloween, Christmas and the like.

A slight smile appeared on Greg's stubbled chin as he pulled into his parking spot, the night already having drawn in, 'What will be will be!'.

Chapter 3
All things Greg

∞∞∞∞∞∞∞∞∞∞∞∞∞∞∞∞∞∞∞∞∞∞∞∞∞∞∞∞∞∞∞∞∞∞∞∞∞∞∞

The grand old age of 49 had arrived – just, he argued, 'just' - but still 49. With this birthday under his belt, where had the decades gone, he quizzed himself. Greg felt that he had hardly looked up from his computer screen from the age of 23, post university, when he had returned home to the family, got a job and, well that was it, he had just worked. Nothing, or more importantly, no one had disturbed him from his changing, and sometimes challenging engineering tasks, as he very slowly moved up the ladder. He had followed his father into the trade, in a different format, electrical engineering of systems, rather than the mechanical engineering that his father had toiled at for 40 odd years for the same employer. The days of one life, one job, one employer were long gone and Greg remembered that this monotony also bought stability, which is what he somehow craved. His attention to detail at work was exact. Very important in engineering to get a project right, but frustrating for his bosses when it came to getting projects completed on time and in budget. These were the sort of pressures that had seen his blood pressure rise of late, with the occasional threat of sacking as a predictable hangover if you failed at your element of the task set.

Greg had stability as he was, in fact he really had everything he desired, as long as he did not want too much. He knew he was never going to set the world alight and was more than comfortable with this. Life was samey, routine, predictable, sedentary, even boring, just the way he would probably order it from life's rich menu.

His real life purchases reflected this, and displayed these attributes, but he had never subscribed to the notion that life would be alone. So here he was, sometimes of the opinion that he was simply looking at the wrong menu! A mid-life crisis perhaps? He would have had to have had a life to have a crisis about it, but he was not convinced by this possibility.

University, in Plymouth, had been great fun, even fulfilling and he achieved the Engineering degree he worked for, with a 2.1. He had had a drunken, and not so drunken encounter or two, and was pleased to have popped his cherry, and if his limited sex life had amounted to a few one-night stands and the odd soft porn film, so be it. His friends had all started out on life's journey and he still had many of these contacts as distant friends. Greg did enjoy the odd evening out with the closest of these, but that was all they were, odd evenings both in timing and in reflection, as their worlds seem to have developed and his had faltered, even stalled.

Annual holiday leave was a problem. Not that it wasn't available, it was just how to spend the time alone. The longer he worked for his employer, the number of days allowance increased. The occasional travel companion came along, and that was usually fun, and an opportunity to be embraced, but in the main, taking a Friday off a month could usually use up a level of his annual leave. Recently, his Friday afternoons had been spent comparing the cost value of dating sites. Reading the terms and conditions was about as much excitement and interest that he was gaining from his performance on the dating scene of late. 'It is all a bit depressing really!' he freely admitted to anyone who was deemed to be a friend enough to share, and share they did on occasion, with the odd observation of who was having what success on what dating site and why. He watched fully committed bachelors crumble before him, whining about the cost of engagement rings or first scan baby pictures appearing on their work cubicle wall. Greg was happy for them, but cried in his heart.

His engineering work was a frustration. Eminently suited to it he knew, but even he found it dull, and the company was more than male dominated, with politically incorrect testosterone filled conversations the norm. The new positive thinking world of understanding, equality, and fulfilment passed them by on the by-pass outside the corroded aluminium windows and as long as none were looking, the two worlds were never likely to collide. Job hopping in his younger work career had not been uncommon. Same work, just a bit more money and some new faces. The faces were different, but somehow the same and there was a carousel of inter-woven business contacts who kept this staff revolve going. Stability, even ambivalence, had overtaken him and even this proposition had changed for Greg. He had stood still, just other colleagues around him changed.

Greg was an unassuming man in stature and nature. His salt and pepper hair had been tightly trimmed with home clippers to save cost and to look respectable, and to hide the ever thinning bald spot and receding temples, although the odd trip to the barbers was afforded every now and then to keep him from looking too DIY. Glasses followed by thirty and a modest salary dictated substance over style. They were bland, as was he, but self-assured in being true to himself. Vanity had also passed him by, which in certain circles would be a good thing, but from a self-maintenance and manicure perspective was a lesson sadly missed.

Keeping fit, almost as a plan to maintain his youth, was important, but it was also a way of absorbing time, that might otherwise be lonely. For him, packing the diary with social contact was a priority, although the interactions seemed shallow. Nevertheless, he continued, almost oblivious to its outcomes.

He rejected religion as an opportunity, but had not searched himself as to why. His parents had dismissed it when he was a child and he did not see the need to challenge this thinking. As the years ticked by, he had touched on the subject, but felt that was just for Christmas, and as the thought occurred in the summer he had time to get round to it, but never did. A suggestion from a friend that church may lead to relationships had kindled his interest, but he backed away and had not returned.

The family remained a constant throughout Greg's time, with ample roasts served on a Sunday, to which you did not have to attend, no obligation (although always implied), but would always make efforts to do so, along with his siblings Gavin and Rebecca and latterly, Mike, Rebecca's fiancé and then husband. Age was no respecter of his parents' health, and his early forties was an adjustment for all the family when they passed away in quick succession. It was if they would last forever, and that was another lie. The estate had left the house to the boys, and the cash to their daughter, Rebecca, who had fled as soon as she reached university, never to return, but now took on the matriarchal duties of the family, with a husband and daughter of her own, and it appeared two big kid brothers also to shepherd.

Rebecca

'I love them and I hate them! How does that work?'. My immature view of my parents as I left my home town in Surrey one September afternoon to move into halls for my university life in Leicester was poor thinking in hindsight. It had been a three year ball, recognized by my dismal degree result, but I was never going to be as academic as my two swotty brothers, so I shall have a life instead! University finished, and with degree in hand, just, work began, love began and a husband was secured. Mike is a great guy and together, we have Gabby, our daughter to love, along with my brothers, the 'kidults' in my life, Gavin and Greg. I miss Mum and Dad now, especially Mum, but I still see my brothers regularly and hope to save them from themselves at some point. It's sort of a life goal to see them happy. It always was, but it seems to be getting harder as we all get more involved in our busy lives of just existing. I'll keep going, you never know and I know Mum would want me to.

For Greg, being an uncle to his niece, Gabby, had been a life highlight. It was fun! A new generation which was not of him, but similar. He loved to be involved, when time allowed, but this had lessened as Gabby had grown from a baby to a girl, now aged 15 going on 27 and already giving him teenage 'feedback' as to why he might be a bit of a geek. It had made him broody at the time, if that was possible for a man, but that time had passed, and so had his opportunity for a family.

He was an ageing nerd and he knew it. 'But nerds were cool...right? But where to now?'.

Living at home, repeat

Greg stayed at his parents' modest, tiring home too long. He knew that, but it was comfortable with usually good food, reliable, flexible if he did have the opportunity to stay out, safe and most importantly, cheap! Sure, he was ribbed by his friends, but the most criticism came from him in wanting to find himself, his purpose, his own space. The inheritance had been welcome. How else was he ever going to get on to the property ladder, a mainstay of the UK psyche, but it also meant that he did not have to do anything, other than to learn loosely how to cook, and you had frozen ready meals for that. Godalming as a town was clean, ageing and above all, quiet.

The post-parent transition had been painful, he freely admitted, and he had at one point hoped he was going to be offered a sympathy fuck at the wake from one of his sister Rebecca's friends who he had always had a crush on, but to no avail. Awkward!

Rebecca and Gavin seemed to adjust better to the loss he felt, and his insular ways seemed to accelerate, as though he was even more lost than he was before. There was little bromance between him and Gavin, sibling rivalries having successfully quashed that years ago. His siblings seemed to accelerate in the other direction, occasionally reaching back to him to drag him forward, although he somehow preferred to languish.

To Greg, dating and coupling up had not been a priority... why would it be? It seemed to be only around the corner, as it was for his parents, but the world had moved on, and even now, he was not really ready. He was a creature of habit and wrongly assumed that this would lead to him finding another lost soul, marry, kids, grow old.

Hopeless? 'No!' he assured himself. 'Hapless? Hmm, I'll give that some thought', as he polished his miniature car collection.

He was not aware of his masculine pride. It never occurred to him, but was there for all to see. The new 'politically correct' world that everyone seemed to refer to had sometimes confounded him, although he did not plan to rally against its purpose. As he understood it, he just wanted to be a part of it, and he felt somewhat isolated from it, and all other aspects of the world.

He found himself questioning every aspect of his life. For someone who was already insular in their outlook, this further recoiled him into the abyss that had become Greg. Was he happy? Should he change? Why? What bloody good would it do anyway? Did he care? Did others really care? The questioning took him to dark places, far from where he had anticipated. Lone walks along the canal were great to share his thoughts with himself, and he tried to use these to free his thinking and his mind.

At one point he had questioned his own sexuality. He understood that most have a point in their life when they do this, and he took some solace from this. But it was not for him, even the thought of it, and that was ok. He was almost pleased with himself that he had even considered the possibility, to liberate himself, and then not to. He had admired the clean living lifestyle that the limited number of gay couples he knew projected. Greg never discussed this possibility with anyone, and even if he had wanted to, there was none close enough to share with, not even his brother.

The raging of testosterone through his body could still be found, if he looked, although that cerebral cupboard was often left out of bounds now as the work pressures of life, and tiredness, made its destination somewhat academic. How could he, would he re-engage this? Once a pressing priority, usually uncontrollably on his zip-fly, those days had dwindled, as had his physical urges. Day to day, he was not sad about this, but some days he mourned the loss of the time when his urge to pro-create may have been settled with someone he loved.

He had grown up in an era when relationships seemed so easy, almost a given...although political correctness was not a known quantity at the time. Only twenty-thirty years ago, it may as well have been the Middle Ages as far as he was concerned.

Pick one at random

Chapter 4
My jeans don't fit!

An adaptive mixture

Mel's work days were usually full on. An adaptive mixture of meetings, emails, presentations, travel around London and the South East, tender documents and graphics. It was interesting, demanding of sorts, and usually meant that she carried the can if the shit hit the fan. She was well known for being decisive in her views, opinions and approach and this was welcomed by most, until they were on the receiving end of any negativity. She did not dish this out regularly or lightly, she had learned that would not get her far, but it usually hurt the recipient when applied. She took no pleasure from this, projects rarely complete themselves and she was usually where the buck stopped in getting these complete.

The team she worked with were younger than her, and she enjoyed this dynamic, preventing any notion that she was 'mother hen', but perhaps an agony aunt instead. Experience was on her side, and she was going to enjoy this advantage. The social side too could be fun, but her clubbing nights were behind her and she usually bailed out after any arranged dinner, before she embarrassed herself by strutting her 90's dance moves on the dance floor. This did not mean that she could not be the life and soul of the party, she surely could, however, Mel was more selective on when and with whom she chose to be the star. Nights in recent years had been filled with books, a semi-regular TV drama catch up on iPlayer, and radio plays when something took her fancy, or just a long drive home from the occasional work seminar.

The first period of time post her separation from Sam had found herself waking up in the middle of the night, still dressed with a once full and now empty bottle of white wine on the coffee table and work in the morning. One evening she had found her favorite pair of jeans from her time with Sam and was furious to discover that they were not even close to fitting any more. Her annoyance had focused her mind on what was piling the pounds on to her once svelte lines, clearly illustrated by her beloved jeans non-fitting stance. The drinking slowed quickly, with the jeans laid carefully over the chair in her bedroom to remind her of the significant target set for fitting them again.

This tangible revelation had focused her mind on other aspects of her life, and a few dark clouds of depression gathered uncomfortably in her thinking.

Mid-Life Crisis

'Why is it still the case that when people talk about a 'mid-life crisis' it's always about bloody men! What about the girls!' she shrieked in her mind. 'I'm having one of my own!' she added to herself. 'Everyone at work brings their cerebral laundry to work and washes it out over lunch in the staff room!' knowing that she was at times guilty of this, but not in sharing her innermost fears and trials, especially the past reliance on alcohol, usually wine, that she was confident she would get under full control sometime soon, just as soon as she finished this current trip down dodgy nostalgia avenue.

Divorces, affairs, separations, dramas, illness, sex and the like were usually in the mix over a typical month at 'Cemetery Junction', as the staff room had fondly become known over the past few years, where you could go to bury all your woes over lunch. Some abstained, until they needed to share this month's catastrophe and put the world to rights in 55 minutes before returning to your desk. The 'system', if that's what it could be called, seemed to have a lifting effect on all the team. It should simply not work, or be allowed, Mel pondered, but it did and it was, if that made sense.

The answers to her now problems, and her recurrent trips into the 'bitter barn' as part of her own crisis with a hangover were not going to be found at the bottom of a wine bottle, and she soon disciplined herself to a no alcohol rule on a 'school-night', unless at an appropriate function. However, this vanilla life she was now leading was, well, dull.

Internet dating

Mel

At first, Mel never took it seriously, although she was a reasonably decisive person and was not in the habit of wasting time on someone that looked pointless. In reality, she actually took internet dating and its filtering of potential mates very seriously if she was to keep the lifeline of sharing her life with someone alive.

Man with his big car, as some form of phallic extension, swipe left, Bearded man with shirt off, swipe left, staged book reading man with uncomfortable looking glasses, swipe left. Mel felt she was in control, just the opportunities seemed endless.....and continually pointless!

'Swiping left all the time, makes your wrist ache after a while' she muttered under her breath as she scrutinized the kaleidoscope of profiles and pictures that were deemed or selected suitable to her.

How does this REALLY work? Should she broaden her search, she thought, or just pick one at random? She had dated a few men that she thought would suit her, to find out they were emotional car-crashes, bi-sexual, clearly out for sex or just married. She had in part gone on looks. Vanity led perhaps? Shallow perhaps? Her choices were clearly not working well as she now realized. 'Dare to swipe right?' Mel whispered to herself.

'Random it is!' she said and swiped right.

'Hmm! Greg…OK! let's see!'.

Greg

'What a muddle!' Fluent in all things internet, Greg's navigation of dating sites was as clumsy as his actual navigation of dating. Technologically adept in all things technology, his inner nerd overcame the Greg to befuddle him. Regularly, swiping right, he chatted back and forth with those that matched his profile and his required profile, although his typed charm was of course lacking.

Internet competition was rife for good dates. Some were on their second, even third marriages....and had no apparent problems in finding love, or what they thought was love. Indeed, this made his task even harder. No fault divorce had just been introduced and the number of newly singled people, it seemed mainly men, had increased in the search for companionship, although for some on the dating sites it was clear that they were only searching for sex. These predators, as he referred to them, which he admitted was a bit harsh, were blatant. He sometimes queried how their offering could work, but some may have found what they were looking for. Each to their own.

Should he change his profile? At least it was honest he thought, still riled over some profiles that were blatant lies, but kept on coming.

'Hang on, contact from a lady called Mel. She seems fun, now don't mess it up again!' as he returned contact and they started to chat.

Mel could not believe what she had done, but went with it to see if it made a difference. The usual swipe right encounters had been real flops, so a random approach might work. A few days passed and with more communications, confidence grew that a date might be worthwhile, although Mel still had reservations on her impulsive 'swipe right'. Greg seemed OK, of sorts, she pondered.

'A meeting? OK!' Mel agreed, although on her terms. Neutral ground, public place, relaxed that it might be a dead end, she agreed to meet the next Saturday evening and if her impulsive swipe right was in fact wrong, she could make an early exit and head home.

Meeting up with Melissa, sorry Mel!

Greg was looking forward to the encounter, although he approached the date with his usual ill-informed and out of character nonchalance to the way he presented himself, both in attire and in spirit. He had thought he had made an effort by putting a dark, off the shelf jacket on, but this was a bit threadbare and showed little physical attention to the crispness that in his mis-guided heart he was trying to portray. Greg was absent at any style classes taken during his teenage years, with his cosseting mother, combined with his sister or older brother, usually in the form of hand-me-downs, dressing him for socials. His older brother was also still single, so clearly any style that they had each shared over time had not been an attraction.

When it came to clothing choice, Greg's social wardrobe was not bursting with combination opportunities. Not a disaster, but lacking in any synergy really to create what can only be described as a poor man's Jeremy Clarkson homage. A good pair of jeans, the 'smart ones', a mid-pair of jeans, relegated from best to middle, having bought new jeans last Christmas. A pair of ironed chinos that had been through the wash with another garment that had left its dulling mark on them, a few casual, mainly plain shirts, one collarless which was his preferred dating shirt, although this fashion died with Grandad, and of course the dark tailored cloth jacket. 'Suitable for all occasions!' in his mind.

Greg's work did not require a suit, just tidy attire and he welcomed this choice. Shoes were sturdy, almost business like, but brown to provide a contrast and then various sets of trainers, tee-shirts and shorts to maintain his exercise routines in its various guises. Of course, underwear was provided by M&S each Christmas and rotated until he could not get away with it anymore!

His brother, Gavin, had more success in relationships than he did, and could be defined as smarter. Confidence as an older brother perhaps? Being asked to stay out at a weekend from his own home as his brother had a 'guest' was rare, but tiresome all the same. He hoped he could 'return the favour' to his brother one day, but he would probably just tell him to piss off! Vanity in clothes, or anything else, was not something that would settle on Greg's CV, but a good man could still be found underneath, if any suitor wanted to find out.

Gavin

Space, that's all I ever wanted. Space from my parents, space from Greg and Rebecca, space at work, just space. I'm really pissed off that the only way I could afford a house was to inherit one, and with Greg of all people, my boring brother. We generally avoid each other if we can, but I know this is in part because we are very similar, which I also know means that I must be a bit boring too, but at least I get more action than he does. Well, actually, that's not very hard really, poor chap. I don't think I cramp his style...do I? Anyway, we're not getting any younger, so each to their own. Sure, if I can help him out, I will, but I'm not going out of my way, I'm too busy!

Gavin was content with his lot, and comfortable in his own skin. Life for him was like a comfy pair of old slippers, and he had no plans to change anytime soon.

Verbal intercourse

Staying the distance in verbal intercourse with women or anyone for that matter, was a fumbled chore for Greg. He was out of touch with one-to-one conversation and sometimes he appeared to be the quiet sort, which he knew he wasn't naturally. Indeed, this was a fair observation as he had never really been one for small talk. The years of being single had only created a cerebral sediment that layered across the social awkwardness that he was not aware of, either in his own home, or with his family.

'Verbal diarrhoea!' was his favourite comment on any prolonged small talk, often cutting this short if he could, sometimes to his surprise as it usually ended the date. He knew he could be purposeful in his conversation, even limited to make his point, then once achieved, stay silent. That was the man, but he also knew that it was limiting in the dating stakes he now engaged in.

Although he lived with his brother, they were like ships in the night, passing occasionally, arguing about who had stolen what from the fridge, but rarely together and never close enough to talk about feelings. That boat had seemed to sail out of harbour when they were children, and its global cruise was lost by the flat earth society.

Although Mel's persona stayed cool about her date on the days approaching on Saturday, she was still mystified as to why she had agreed to the date with Greg, in Byfleet, which she sort of knew, and in the same breath, she was intrigued to see if she had in fact uncovered some hidden gem of a chap, who just needed rescuing from himself, or his family, or both! Her mind said she had not, but her heart was telling her to go with it. 'Heart over mind every time!' she thought, although she would be pretty pissed off if it turned out that she should have gone with her mind.

Chapter 5
Date night in Byfleet

'Just remind me why you swiped right?', Mel questioned herself as she made herself ready for her date. On the one hand she was intrigued about Greg, finely balanced by the consistent thought that she may have made a terrible error and was going to meet a nerd, but just not any nerd, but a super-nerd! She almost wanted it to fail, but there was so much failure before with other dates that she wanted it to work. If she kept trying the same type of people and not finding what she was looking for, she needed to change the 'ingredients', and she had never really tried a geek before? But there was just something that she could not really identify in Greg that she wanted to check out.

'Will it work?', Mel questioned herself again, brushing her hair whilst remembering the Thursday night before when she had typed out a message to cancel, but just couldn't quite bring herself to press send, having received a few 'diss-cards' as she called them herself in the past. 'Dress down a bit' she thought, so as not to arouse him too much if he is what she suspects.

Mel had made the effort to meet up with Greg by travelling across from South London in her small, and slightly tired black hatchback. Mel, as she always did on a first date, wanted the security of knowing she could leave at a moment's notice, back to the sanctuary of her flat should this Greg turn out to be somewhat over-descriptive of the illusion that was him. The large and reasonably full pub car park was easily found. Mel waited in the car for a few minutes to ready herself and then headed to the bar, where she was certain she or he would recognize each other, as long as they had been honest.

The drive to the venue was not long for either of them, just to the edge of the M25 motorway, to an ageing chain gastro-pub that they both vaguely knew and gave the comfort of knowing that they knew their respective ways home if it was not to be. The season was changing, but still warm in the evenings and both dressed lightly, ignoring the chance of rain or chill.

The bar was as she vaguely remembered it, to her disappointment; just everything was a little more faded and the carpets a lot more tacky. She gave a quick glance across the pub and soon spotted Greg. Her heart dropped a beat as she saw that he was exactly as anticipated and she muttered 'swipe left 'to herself and looked down for a second to avoid eye contact. He was in an open booth close to the other end of the rather long bar and she pulled herself together, placed a fake smile on her face and headed over to introduce herself, preferably with some confidence she thought, but also in the hope that she was wrong about him. Had her hunch that he was ok failed? Her stride faltered slightly as she headed down the bar and the glimpse of the toilets gave her one additional opportunity to compose herself.

She nipped to the toilet to make sure she was ready for the encounter, Mel checked her hair in the water-splattered mirror of the white tiled wall and headed for her first encounter with her impulse 'swipe right' date.

The back of the toilet door had a hand-written crayon notice which read:

Are you on a date that isn't working out?

Is your Tinder or PoF date not who they said they were on their profile?

Does it all feel a bit weird?

Do you feel like you're not in a safe situation?

Go to the bar and ask for Tina. Our team will know you need some help getting out of the situation without much fuss.

She pondered this as she headed to the booth for the meeting with Greg. In a way she was hoping that Greg was not going to turn out to be the 40+ year old virgin he portrayed. Clearly a pub for dating, she was reassured that the bar staff knew there could be problems and were in part ready to stand in if things went wrong.

Sam, her ex, had explained a couple of years back that she could text him any time when dating to say, 'get me out' and they had agreed he would call one minute later to say there was an emergency and she had to come home, if needed. Mel was miffed when she had used the system once and Rupert had called rather than Sam. She was comforted that someone was there, just a bit upset that it was the rather effeminate Rupert doing the protecting, rather than Sam. Rupert could be such a drama queen and she could do without that if there was a real emergency.

'Here goes!' echoed in her mind as she approached her date.

Greg was ready and stood to shake hands and smiled before asking 'Melissa, sorry, Mel, hello, I'm Greg!'. He smiled awkwardly as he beckoned her to the small booth he had occupied, ready for the date.

'Shall we go halves on the drinks?' asked Greg, followed by, 'What can I get you?'. She smiled, hiding a slight grimace at what could be a mistake. Greg was no looker and his tired clothes let him down, reinforcing Mel's view that this was not going to be a great, or long, night out.

'Did you find it, the pub, ok?'.

'Sure, it seems like a nice place!' Mel smiling as she made eye contact and lying to herself. He blushed.

'It is, I've been loads of times!', Greg exclaimed, before backtracking, 'Not for dates, well, with friends, it's close to a nice walk along the canal. You happy to sit here, we can go to the bar if you prefer?', changing the topic promptly as his nerves ran ahead of him.

'This is fine, thanks.' She reassured him, as she sat down, having removed her fleece top as the evening was still warm.

Greg hesitated, admiring Mel as she settled, before remembering himself.

'Can I get you a drink? You get the next round?'.

'Thanks, Diet Coke please, I'm driving'.

'Cool, give me a minute', he smiled as he pulled his brown leather wallet from his dark jacket and purposefully lunged, slightly nervously, to the bar.

Mel looked around the pub, which was doing a brisk trade, but quiet with its darker decor and mood lighting. Greg seemed as he described, which was a disappointment and relief at the same time, a bit more mousey than she had anticipated, but far better than some others she had met. She could stay for a drink, maybe two, but she would let it roll for now. She looked out of the window for the reassurance that her car was there, just in case.

Greg was pleased with his casual introduction. It took a lot for him not to fuck it up on first sight, and he turned and smiled at Mel as the drinks arrived.

Two tall, frost-clad glasses appeared, a Diet Coke and an orange J2O were placed on the table and Greg tucked himself back into the tight booth, returning the eye contact to Mel, in his best 'I can do this' type way. Mel took the opportunity to check his wedding ring finger for any tell-tale marks as the drinks were placed before her, although she already knew he was not married by his boyish appearance and the dress sense of a confirmed bachelor. A nerd evolves and is not created through marriage, and Greg so far was as described.

'I'm driving too!' he smiled, asking what car she drove in an awkward attempt to get the conversation going.

'It's black!' is all she wanted to offer, shutting him down. 'Have you had a good day?' wanting to get to the point of the rendezvous, which was to know Greg better.

'Yeah!' he said with some enthusiasm, before detailing what to Melissa sounded like a rather tedious, male-orientated pursuit bound day before finding himself in the pub with Mel on a Saturday night.

Mel listened, her interest in Greg ebbing at his every sentence. When he stopped, there was an awkward pause. He did not ask about her day, so, she started chatting about what she had been up to. Admittedly, it was not that exciting either, but she felt that if she didn't take the lead, the conversation and date was going to be super short.

Greg knew he should have asked, but got tongue tied, as he had on many occasions. He listened intently, missing any cues to interact. Melissa kept going until the conversation rather fizzled out.

Greg smiled, close to grimacing, as the drinks ran dry at about the same time.

'Can I get you another?', he offered, hoping to bridge the pregnant pause.

'No, it's actually been a long day, longer than I had thought, and still lots to do. I'm going to cut and run if I may, but it's been great to meet you finally'.

'I was hoping we could get something to eat?' he suggested, hoping that this was not going to be another fail he could notch on his loser board of nerd-dom.

'No! I'm good, but thanks'. She raised her hand to shake his whilst also reaching for her fleece, 'Great to meet up though', and then left the booth to return to her car.

The drive home was slow. It had started to rain and the windscreen wipers danced in front of her, with the traffic slowing to the conditions, as she made her way to the main roads and home.

Mel pondered the encounter on her way home. Greg had been OK. He seemed fine really, but just boring. A boy in a man's clothing, a bit eager to tell her about Greg's world, and not a great listener. She could do better than him, couldn't she? Or did she not take long enough to really find out. A pang of guilt passed her mind as she pulled away from the traffic lights and pulled into her car park. Oh well, there will be another chance, plenty more fish...she stopped. Hmmm!

Greg sat back in the booth and watched her exit the pub, his heart sinking as he felt his heart pump its blood to his now blushing cheeks. He saw her black car pull out of the car park, the rain highlighted in her headlights. He checked his mobile, but no messages from anyone. He knew this, it was almost a nervous reaction to check. The date had started averagely, and sort of fizzled out from there. At least she had turned up, which had not always been the case.

Greg looked around the pub as he pondered this latest failure. He was not normally an overly emotional man, but he wanted to sob. He peered into his now empty drink glass; some of the conversations around him were loud, in one case as though they wanted the whole world to know of their conquests, and errors.

The next booth held two men, both in their mid-thirties, comparing notes on their recent dating experiences, clearly free from their respective partners, for a while anyway:

'So, I was a bit unsure about this date. I thought she looked really great on her profile, and she did when we met up. It was just the deeper voice and large hands that gave it away. I don't do trans, but she was great to chat to. 'I had to address the elephant in the room' he declared, 'We went on to dinner, but I wasn't going further!' he said in a loud, jovial voice.

His friend piped up, 'You know that girl I have been dating, the younger one?'.

'Yes, nice, didn't she get a bit heavy with you about family and commitment and all that stuff?'

'Yeah, that's the one! Well, I sort of obliged!'.

'What!', he almost shouted in disbelief.

'Yeah, she's pregnant…3 months!'.

'But you haven't left your wife yet, you pillock!'.

Their voices at this point hushed somewhat at their revelations and Greg tuned out accordingly.

He smiled and looked up, a 'not doing that badly then' look on his face. A younger couple were in an opposite booth in the corner, next to the toilets. He thought they were a couple, as their faces were fully conjoined with each other's, his medium beard almost consuming her pale face leading to her long blonde hair. Their heightened amorous state was only just controlled, as his hands danced across the top of her thigh and across her blouse heading to rest on her shoulder, pausing at the contours of her breasts for just a little too long.

Greg tried not to stare as they seemed to pause, have a drink, share some conversation, a joke or two and then start again. It was almost as though they were sea mammals coming up for air after a deep dive, before returning to the depths of lust for each other.

He returned his gaze to his empty glass, the disappointment of Mel leaving so early returning to him head on, and realising that he had been staring at the couple, although he thought the spectacle was going to get out of control at one point, a reddened blush to his face now clear for all to see, with 'get a room' ringing in his mind.

Mel seemed nice, very nice, and his chest deflated at the thought of another failure. 'Must learn to listen' he chastised himself, as he swooshed what remained of the J2O around in the now melted ice in his empty glass, and took the remaining sip. He could get a take away curry for one on the way home, he thought. 'I think F1 race highlights will be on, in HD as well!'. It was little consolation for his original plans, and Mel was a loss he would find troubling to reconcile.

He stood up from the booth and popped his jacket on. As he left, his place was taken instantly at the booth by another loved-up young couple, and he acknowledged the landlord as he left to say thanks, while his walk to his car was deliberately slow. It was as if he wanted to get wet in the now pouring rain to rinse him of whatever was wrong with him, whatever made Mel, and others, switch off. Such immediate rejection was tough, but always a possibility.

The car door clunked behind him and Greg took his jacket off and laid it on the front seat before sitting behind the wheel of his car. He sat silent for a minute or two and the windows steamed up inside accordingly. He started the car, put the windscreen wipers and fan on blast and drove home. Anyway, the rain would at least give him an excuse to wash the car tomorrow, he tried to cheer himself, and afterwards lunch with Rebecca, Gabby and Mike. Great! But he knew it was not.

Pick one at random

Chapter 6
Hello Sarah! Goodbye Sarah!

Mel had somehow been different to his other dates and encounters. She had somehow mesmerized him, not in a sexual way, but just by her gentle, confident style that was simple and feminine. He had found the following few weeks difficult in adjusting his thoughts of what could have been with Mel, and now was not. Greg did not want to give up on the embers of hope that were his love life, as he nearly had a few times before, and his erstwhile optimism kept him clicking on the various dating sites he subscribed to on the internet to find a match.

Greg now regularly updated his profile with better pictures, or enhanced descriptions to make himself more appealing. Well he hoped so! Rebecca, his sister and at his request, had viewed a few of his listings to see if there was anything to add or take away. She found it rather cringeworthy, and had asked to stop when Mike, her husband, had become concerned, if not slightly insecure, that she was frequently visiting dating sites. More hopeful but ultimately pointless dates followed, rarely getting to an exchange of mobile numbers, let alone a second date. Internet introduction or otherwise, ending on the first night with a shared meal ticket and a handshake were the norm. He did not want more failure, it just found him...regularly. Just to find someone he could bind with in his mind and share his life, however mundane he knew he could be, was all he wanted. He thought of Mel for a moment, and then moved on.

Saturday nights seemed to be the time for dating, and he found himself heading for a rendezvous with Sarah at a Morden bar, well known on the dating scene as a safe haven, but handy to meet equidistant from her home in Putney, and his on the outskirts of Godalming. Well, as Greg calculated, it was sort of equidistant, with Greg covering more miles, which he seemed pointlessly to want to clearly note, had he had the chance. Arriving in advance, the bar had a relaxed vibe and he spotted Sarah as she had also arrived early, but she did not even stay for a drink. She at least apologised nicely, saying an emergency had arisen, and with a smile had left almost immediately. His inner heightened mojo for the evening ebbed quickly from his soul.

The year, thus far, was not proving to be a vintage year for Greg in the dating stakes. Indeed, the last few years of his 'harvest' had turned to an unpalatable vinegar. And where his hope had in the early years been an advantage, dating was now a chore, and his tolerance to continue ebbed further. How could he not take it so personally? His faith in himself as a good man was falling, as it was in the light trust that he placed in the dating sites he frequented. Surely a perfect companion was out there, possibly looking for him?

Melissa, hello!

Greg sighed. He normally at least got to a second Diet Coke, having driven to a date, but the conversation and introduction had died on its feet from the moment they met, and Sarah had made her excuses and left before he could offer her a Prosecco or the like. 'Swipe left' he uttered under his breath, as he suddenly felt decidedly awkward at the busy bar alone.

He gathered his thoughts and composed himself from his almost immediate rejection. Greg paid for his drink, ordered whilst sequencing what had gone wrong with Sarah, confirming it was over before he had been party to the involvement, and gathered his jacket. He took a glance around the unfamiliar bar, and was aware that he was not exactly alone in his experience. A familiar face in the form of Mel was at a table across the room and mirrored his demeanor.

He paused, even hesitated, trying to fathom how she could be at the same destination, and then remembering the dating sites map locator of safe venues for first dates and encounters. He headed to the door, passing her table. 'Hi Melissa, sorry, Mel, you OK?' he asked, more out of concern for her, than any opportunity that might be on the cards. Mel shared his slightly bewildered stare, a first date having just left. 'Hi...Greg! What are you doing here?'.

'I'm just leaving, another failed internet date and I'm hungry!', Greg confirmed, continuing to move towards the door. 'Oh! Hi...um...want to go halves?', she hesitated for a second, then smiled.

'Sure!', Greg not really realising he had just secured a second date, indicating to the bar door, as he opened it and ushered Mel out to the night, coats and jackets in hand. The town streets were busy, and he had researched a place round the corner if his date had gone well. He was hungry and the menu looked good value, so he would head there anyway, now with Mel.

Mel had dressed for her original date in dark blue jeans, black leatherette ankle boots, flowing cream blouse loosely buttoned, and lacy black bra, highlighted below the blouse. Foundation, blush, heavy mascara and lip-gloss applied, she still radiated confidence, although this had been a little dented by the encounter with her planned date. Terry seemed older by about 15 years than his description. She should have guessed by his name, and his sun tan gave away his wedding ring mark on his finger, clearly freshly removed and probably in the top pocket of his ghastly Hawaiian style shirt. His eagerness to go to a local hotel within the first five minutes had met with a flat refusal and he had left like a scolded child when it became clear that he was not going to score with Mel that night. This is the point where Greg had passed by and said hi.

Her nude-colour bomber style jacket was fitted and complemented both her outfit and her hair, recently cut in preparation for her date. As they entered the restaurant, Greg absorbed all that he could of her form, rather excited, and somehow bewildered, that he was sharing dinner with her, the woman that had beguiled him all those weeks back.

The seating choice at the restaurant was mutual, and they shared a cosy table, ordering noodles and a small light beer each. The instantaneous, unplanned nature of the encounter was unlike both of them, and was somehow outside their comfort zone, but they felt strangely familiar, even comfortable with each other.

Things in common

They had no perception that they had anything in common, but that changed as they dined and shared their pasts together. From current life, to growing up in a 70s-80s family, to hating Marmite, to space-hoppers, anti-Brexit, to trying smoking and never picking up another cigarette again, to liking Def Leppard, hot curries, to keeping in shape, to Star Wars over Star Trek, Tolkien over Rowling, to Domino's pizza over Nando's chicken, the synergy became even more telling. Greg was getting the handle of this small-talk and it seemed effortless with Mel. Even their work, for which they tried to limit conversation, seemed to have comparisons, although they were unrelated industries, in the pressures that needed to be coped with and shouldered.

Relaxed, sharing, caring, understanding, laughing, considering all hovered over the conversation as they ate. Anyone observing would have thought they were a long standing item. Both Mel and Greg would grasp quickly afterwards that what they were looking for was in front of them. Their mutual sub-conscious over-rode their reservations as they conversed like old, long lost friends would.

Eye contact seemed almost constant as they engaged in banter, like a newly married husband and wife that share the day's events with each other over the evening meal at the dinner table at home. Two hours had ticked by with much engaged spontaneity and shared wry humor at their dating downfalls and disasters, their shortest dates and the lying profiles they had discovered, neither in a hurry to get home to empty abodes, with many laughs during the evening as they compared base notes on their failures to find what they were looking for.

The bill arrived, and they shared the cost before heading for the car park, Greg offering Mel his coat as an addition to her own jacket as the cool evening air struck them from the warm restaurant. She was fine and they realized their cars were in the same location as it transpired where they had both parked, just on different levels.

'I'm sorry I dashed off when we last met. It won't happen again!', Mel confirmed gazing into his eyes, as she had found herself comfortably doing for most of the conversation. She gave him a warm look, almost at peace with herself, with a friend she had known for years, but had only just discovered and their surprise night ended with a peck on the cheek from Mel and a light embrace, although it was clear to them both that they were comfortable to pursue more time together.

'You know we mentioned Star Wars?', Greg blurted.

'Yes!', she looked slightly surprised with this curve ball response.

'Special screening next Friday night in Tolworth, if you'd like to go…no dashing off mind!', he offered, confidently grinning as he seized the opportunity, but still concerned he might be rejected.

'Cool! Love to!' Mel confirmed, leaning forward to give him another kiss on his stubbly cheek, this time a little slower than before. 'Speak in the week, and dinner after OK?', giving Greg her number as she turned and headed for her car, a slight lift in her step as she reached the car. The tube lighting kept her figure in view and Greg admired her form as she turned, waving to him as he stood unmoving from their gentle end encounter, indicating that she would call him. He watched her drive away, Greg giving a thumbs-up as she passed, relishing in part the thought of getting her black car washed and polished.

Greg was touched by Mel's warm charm instantly. His waking hours would be full of Mel, and something welcome, inspiring even, over the coming week would just not leave him alone. Mel had somehow been stand-offish at their first meeting, keen to disengage, but the unguarded persona beneath the veneer had been beguiling to observe.

Mel also found herself distracted by what had happened, those few hours over a bowl of noodles and chicken, with Greg, who was perhaps not so boring after all. Their time together had been so light, so easy, so warm, but with a person who she hardly knew anything about, geeky as he was, but was now compelled to know more. Could she dream, should she dare to dream?

Awkward silence!

Melissa's experience of following up a date was limited. To be honest, she had not really met anyone worth following up, but was adept at rejecting unwelcome advances where she needed to. This was tiring, even boring, and therefore her desire to follow up her contact with Greg was heightened. She had a fair view that he was slightly backwards in coming forwards and that making a move would need to be achieved with some respect to his pride. Archaic thinking she smiled, but she too was at heart a traditionalist and could understand how he might feel.

Mel's intuition also observed that he may not be familiar with the art of arguing. Why would he be, other than sibling arguing with Gavin, his brother, his social contact with women was limited, and Rebecca his sister did not count, well that's what Greg told himself anyway, and his interaction with a partner in a relationship even more so. Head on disagreements she felt, if they arose, were unlikely to see anything other than a shutdown, 'can't compute' situation with Greg reverting to a scolded child, rather than a mature adult debate. She was OK with this, noting that she had been known in the past to be confrontational, and if she wanted to progress with Greg, this loveable geek, and she did, she would control herself, rather than be controlled.

The exchange of texts and calls grew during the week as their friendship and styles began comfortably to align.

Simply to be loved by an equal. Was there one?

Greg had not been brought up to believe that the man should take the lead and be the head of the household. It just was there! This stereotype had been correctly challenged in so many ways, becoming ever more vocal in recent times, particularly through the social media channels he connected to. Greg was a willing recipient to respect these modern and long overdue views, indeed he always thought of himself in being quite liberal in his approach on most evolutions of changing perception in the new world that was occurring. It put a whole enlightened perspective on the way he observed and interacted with his fellow beings, where he could. However, in other respects, he felt that some of the tide had moved too quickly for him, and certainly occurred after his formative years of yesteryear, and the typical nuclear family of 2.4 kids, a detached house, Cortina on the drive, Dad as the breadwinner, and Mother the loving glue that stuck their tiny universe together. And he missed it! Not the structure, just the love!

His liberal opinions had been challenged by what appeared to be the onslaught of views that mid-aged man, usually middle class living in comfortable suburbia, was the cause of many of society's ills and that they, including him, must, must, must be corrected at all costs with new thinking. Greg had enough problems of his own to think about, and with this perceived view of his place in society, he found that keeping himself to himself, silent, offered some safe passage, even if this was alone. 'Each to their own and wish them well, but don't judge me!' and 'Opinions are great, opinionated is not!' was his view.

Personal confidence

Mel normally brimmed with confidence, until it came to being intimate with someone. This had not always been the case, especially with Sam. Indeed, she had once been the experimenter in the bedroom, but her love betrayal had been complete and it remained with her.

Greg had always struggled in all areas of confidence, unless it was some tedious engineering challenge. Confidence had been all but been crushed out of him personally and time had not been kind in helping recover this position. He felt that this was because he had never had anyone to love, to trust, to share in the way that adults do. And he wanted that more than anything, although he would never confide that reality to anyone, well not yet anyway.

Together, over noodles and beer, confidence had fitted them both like a well-worn cardigan that had held them in its structure. Both Mel and Greg had not felt so at ease for years and in Greg's case for decades. This was not love at first sight. It was more explosive than that, emotional dynamite that had had the detonator implanted by the skillful hands of them both, with neither of them understanding the instructions, but getting a 'Wow!' from their shared time together. Their confidence in each other was only matched by the shared uprising of confidence in their own self and it warmed them both. They had to be together again, and soon.

Star Wars, the next encounter...well almost!

The working week could not pass fast enough for them both. A few calls were made to confirm the arrangements, although the planned film was fully booked. They would still go to the cinema, just not for the inter-galactic feast they had first planned. Mel's preferred choice was in fact horror films, but she was not sure Greg was up for that and the latest incarnation of Star Wars could wait for another date if needed.

They were adults now, they could do what they wanted, and they could see each other tonight, or any night, if they wanted. There were no rules, no parents to stop them, or perceived curfew to observe. Somehow, this time getting it right was important, vital, to take each step as it arrived with reverence and care, both already caring for each other in their minds. The cinema as a date seemed a bit corny and old school to Mel. She did not think they were going there to snog like teenagers, although she did hope that this might create a colourful interlude to what looked like a tedious film, but she knew that to Greg it was his approach to dating her. She was cool with that, indeed there were no rules, although she also knew that the world had moved on a few decades since his youth.

Greg was surprised, if not delighted at himself. It was like being with a friend who he had known all his life, but only just knew. Mel felt secure with Greg, their closeness accelerating with each encounter. She even tucked his shirt in to stop him trying to look trendy, and felt good touching him so closely, almost mothering him, but in a personal way, something she had not done for years. They smiled at each other and Greg gave her a warm kiss on the cheek, 'Thank you!', he whispered as he smiled at her and moved to buy tickets at the cinema. His tired aftershave filled her nostrils, and it warmed her. 'Need to change that!' She thought, but he had not recoiled from the close attention, and her heart skipped at the thought that her engineering nerd might just be ok....or more!

The film was rubbish, cringeworthy indeed, which in itself made it amusing. They would go again another time to see their first choice epic and it was the best of a bad batch on show that night and they both knew it. The desire just to be together was sufficient to endure the tedious plot as it unravelled. The popcorn seemed cheesy, and being rather stale, it even tasted cheesy at one point, although they both happily chomped through the contents of the paper bucket as the flick wound on. Melissa took his hand and held it for what seemed to be the duration of the film, but was only the last 20 minutes. Her hand was gentle and just held his with calm firmness. He felt his heart rate rise, but then subside as its natural occurrence became apparent. He worried he would sweat too much and make the encounter clammy, but he was cool for the duration.

As the credits rolled, she leant across and gave him a kiss on his cheek. 'Thank you' she smiled, as they both rose and laughed on their way out of the auditorium at how truly shit the film had been.

'Just going to stop to ask for my money back' he jested as they left the cinema and entered the night sky.

'Greg?', Mel asked.

'Hmm?', he responded, as he patted his jacket to ensure he had wallet, phone and keys.

'Can I see you before next weekend please' she asked, having turned to face him.

'Um, great, sure…when?' caught slightly unawares, but pleased at the same time.

'Can I call you tomorrow? Dinner, at mine?'.

'Oh! Let me think' he continued his jesting, nodding wildly, before she stopped him with a kiss on his lips. Greg was spellbound and held her gently as they embraced. He could not wait!

Chapter 7
Dash to dinner

Greg's sister, Rebecca, spoke to her brothers by phone every week, almost like an unwritten ritual continued on from their late folks. This was usually followed up with lunch once a month where diaries allowed, on a Sunday for roast to replicate her mother's good work over their formative years. As the honorary mother figure, she had pledged to herself that she would look after her brothers when their parents had passed away. Greg was at home when she called, usually on a Wednesday after work, and with tea in hand his mobile had rung. He grabbed it with hope that it would be Mel, although he hid his disappointment from Rebecca.

Her woman's intuition kicked in quickly when she spoke to Greg. He seemed more relaxed, confident and, unusual for him, almost excitable of late, and she knew that there was a change, a positive one, in his demeanour. Rebecca was never shy in stepping into the breach in guiding what she still viewed as her mis-guided brothers, and she steered the conversation round to all things Greg quickly. He sensed this was coming, in fact he was bursting to share his new-found interest, but had little control of the conversation, as was ever the case when it came to female verbal intercourse. She loved both her brothers, and to have some gossip about them was almost as exciting for her as it was for Greg.

'So, you seem a bit different in the last few weeks, anything you want to share?' she probed.

'Different? Um, no, no, just busy at work, as ever' he stumbled. Rebecca knew he was bluffing.

'OK! Good, great to hear you're busy. Who are you busy with?'.

'...just work, a big project on, it's a bit boring really!', vainly trying to head the thread away. Rebecca was having none of it!

'Greg!' with a slightly stern voice, 'What's her name please', guessing this was his new distraction.

'Ah! Um, well...can I hold off that please until later?', Greg clearly squirming at the end of the line.

'Name!'.

'Mel!', he blurted...Melissa, Mel.

'Thank you! Wonderful! Tell me all about Mel?'.

Greg was light on the detail. By nature, both he and Rebecca knew he was not going to be the most engaging when it came to describing a new rare belle, but even taking into account the shortfalls that characterized Greg, she could feel that his heart had been lifted. She issued some cheeky words of advice, empathy, sibling banter, to goad him, but also for him to know that she approved and he could call anytime if he needed any guidance.

'...and don't forget to buy her flowers. She'll like that and for flip's sake, make sure you make her laugh every now and then. Do you need me to send you your M&S undies early this year for Christmas?', she quipped at the end of her sentence.

'Thanks for the advice and no to the undies', knowing that he would need to update the current underwear.

'Best way to get her into bed!'.

'Rebecca please!' Greg retorted, but not objecting in truth.

She laughed loudly 'Love you, speak soon', signing off before hanging up, much to the relief of Greg in getting away relatively unscathed and hoping that Mel would contact soon.

His mobile went quiet and his soul was full, relieved that he had shared his happy burden with another, although he also knew the update would be leaked to his older brother, Gavin, who would implement the Spanish Inquisition at the earliest opportunity. And he did within a few days, one evening on his return from a tiring day, with overtime thrown in. He had put up little resistance that night towards the end of the same week, eating a microwave warmed pasty for dinner, and then heading for his bed.

Greg settled on his sofa in the lounge, his now cooling tea on the side table and he texted Mel, neither of them having much time that day to communicate.

'Hi! Just thinking of you. How's today been for you?', pressing send and reaching for his tea.

'Worn out! Are you home?', his phone chirped.

'Yes!'.

'Have you eaten yet? Just about to cook dinner, can make it for two if you leave now?', Greg beamed, his fingers could not type fast enough.

'On my way, postcode and number please!'. He could wait for the response in the car, as he grabbed his car keys, wallet, house keys and jacket and leapt for the door and his journey.

His mobile chirped with the address and he entered the details into his sat-nav at the petrol station as he approached the motorway, taking Rebecca's advice to buy flowers, although he had to admit that they looked a bit droopy and limp. He shrugged his shoulders to the pathetic choice, and grabbed a bunch, with a discounted bottle of wine to boot. 'Not going empty handed!' he pondered to himself, as he pressed his card on the electronic pad to pay and sprinted back to the car.

The 25 minutes' drive was an excited blur, as he turned his music up, interrupted occasionally by the sat nav telling him to turn right, turn left and at one point to turn around! 'Piss off!' he shouted angrily at the screen as he made a spirited U-turn and took the next junction to get back on course.

He found Mel's apartment, noting the black car he had seen before outside. Greg wore his obligatory open neck collarless casual shirt. It was slightly different, outdated indeed, but he liked the variance that to the observant showed a small amount of style, mainly covered by his usual dark jacket. His brown sensible shoes certainly did not differentiate, and as he had aged, comfort over style seemed to be have become his mantra.

He rang the entry buzzer, and Mel answered. 'Excellent timing, come in, first floor, Number Six' she instructed, as the door release sounded and Greg re-gathered the flowers and wine and headed for the stairs. Number Six. He tapped on the wood coloured door.

'It's open' a faint voice could be heard and he wandered in, the tempting smell of cooking hitting him instantly as Mel greeted him in the lobby.

'Hi!' she smiled, leaning in to kiss him gently on the cheek, but close enough to his mouth to be more than just a guest greeting. The scent of her perfume overcame the cooking smells and he was lost, just for a moment. Greg responded by giving her a gentle, if not hesitant kiss on the lips, Mel looked him in the eyes, her eyebrows raised appreciatively, being pleased with this in reinforcing their mutual positions as their relationship deepened. Greg was not familiar with being that forward and his heart raced, he smiled and handed her his gifts.

'Flowers, thank you and wine, fab! Should go well with the chicken, although I shouldn't on a school night!' she smiled, taking the flowers and disappearing into the kitchen from the small lobby.

'Chicken OK for you?', she questioned in a raised voice.

'Cool, I'm starving!' he smiled, she somehow knowing that he would be. Their various encounters had usually involved food of some description and he always seemed to be hungry.

'Good! Can you get the wine open please?'.

'Sure!' as he scouted the neat apartment to get his bearings on what room was where and the potential location of a bottle opener. He felt relaxed almost instantly. A quiet radio broadcasted what sounded like a play, or the finale of it, from the room ahead, that looked like the living room, with bedrooms to the right, he was interrupted from the kitchen.

'Go straight ahead for the lounge, loo is on the left if you need it!', a relaxed but clearly busy Mel confirmed from the kitchen, plates clanking as they were being laid out to serve. 'The bottle opener is on the table!' she added.

The table in the living room was set for dinner for two, wine glasses ready and sofa looking comfy. The lights were slightly dimmed and the radio was now playing jazz softly in the corner, providing a relaxed mood, rather than romantic. The cork popped from the bottle and he poured two small glasses of wine, as Mel entered the lounge, plates in hand.

Dinner shifted around various topics and banter. They were both hungry after a long day at their respective offices and both warmed to the oasis of opportunity to be together at Mel's home. Mel wanted to know more about Greg, their time together in the noodle restaurant had been mesmeric and she wanted to understand what made him tick a little bit further to ensure that he was the nice guy that she thought he was, rather than some secretive axe swinging murderer from leafy Godalming. She had never heard of one, and was confident that Greg was the special nerd she thought he was.

His powers of debate had been somewhat hidden over the years, preferring an easier life to any controlled confrontation that may occur. More than hidden, they were also rusty, with none to share his innermost thoughts and secrets with. That did not mean that he did not have strong views or ethics on various important topics. It just meant that he was not going to get on a soap-box about any of them, and never had. Mel was endeared by his naivety, almost as though he needed to be rescued, but then to be loved, nurtured and held.

It was clear that Mel had a stronger passion for conversation than Greg, for views, for debate, for most things. She wanted more than ever to reveal Greg for who he really was, although the process was at times proving frustrating. She understood that you should never really discuss politics, religion, past relationships, so she thought she would press each button of Greg's to see what fell out, almost like a '20 questions' session, not wanting it to turn into an interrogation but to enhance her growing belief that Greg, her swipe right geek, was to be her new love. She would rather know now, than wait to find out he was just a nerd, rather than the real, caring but rather undiscovered man that her intuition suggested he was. It felt like it by the time she had finished her interrogation, with the lights slightly dimmed, the process felt like a film set of a police interview.

Brexit was highly topical, and Mel went for it.

'Where do you think the UK is with Brexit?', she asked, head on.

'I can't understand why they called a Referendum in the first place. It seemed to answer a question that very few were asking'.

'The original Government White Paper was rubbish, so I voted to stay in. The vote says we have to leave, but on such shit terms seems ridiculous. So I think we are heading in the wrong direction to answer the question. We should have had this sorted by now and I am not reading the 585-page deal document!', he smiled, knowing that it was a contentious and highly emotional issue for most.

'And you?' he responded.

'I agree, a right mess!', Mel responded, pleased that Greg had been confident to have a view he could share and have a balanced knowledge on the topic.

'OK, are you religious?'.

'No!', stated Greg abruptly, 'And you?' he enquired in return. She shook her head promptly.

'When's the last time you had a girlfriend?' Mel asked.

Greg blushed and recoiled slightly. 'About a decade', he confirmed, embarrassed by his answer. She touched his hand briefly, before reaching for her glass.

'And you?', to deflect his response.

'About 4 years ago, Sam was his name. I thought we would live happily ever after, meringue wedding, and all that! Hmm!', she returned.

'Still miss him?', Greg could see that she clearly still did.

'Yes and no. I miss the company, the friendship, the fun, but not the conflicts when they came...' she stopped herself and looked away.

Greg aimed to lighten the mood by sensing that a change of subject might be in order. 'I'm going to need to stop drinking wine now, I will need to drive home, work in the morning', he sighed.

'Why don't you stay over and have another one?' she asked. 'You can stay in the second bedroom, I'm not going to jump you, well not tonight anyway!', Mel smiled, with such a look of confidence that she could do just that.

Greg hesitated for a second, immediately thinking of the practicalities that he had not brought a change of clothes, then he stopped himself, 'Grow a pair will you!' he asserted his inner self.

'You can try and jump me, but seriously, if I can be gone by 7am, I can get to work and stay over tonight. It would be nice to be with you' as he reached for the wine with a wry grin, hoping that he had not gone too far, and poured them both another glass.

'Sofa time?', Mel indicating the brown sofa way from the dinner table. 'I'll clear up the table tomorrow when you leave'.

'Cool!', he smiled with some relief, not knowing how this was all going to work, but clearly relishing the opportunity to discover a more un-coordinated, dis-organized side to himself that he was unfamiliar with.

He loved it!

Pick one at random

Chapter 8
Box room?

With the hours ticking by, Mel gave Greg some space to make himself comfortable in the small box room, confirming that he could get a shower in the morning. 'Thanks!' he smiled. He looked tired and leant forward and gave her a small, but tender loving kiss. 'See you in the morning', before readying for bed.

He made himself at home and his bedroom light went out soon afterwards. She cleared the table quietly and after a few minutes poked her head round the corner of his room to ensure he was comfortable and had all he needed. The hall light crept into the darkened room and he was already asleep. 'Night Greg' she whispered softly. He stirred slightly, before snorting somewhat and then resuming his slumber. He was very still and his breathing soft.

His phone, watch, keys, glasses and wallet were placed symmetrically on the bedside cabinet, jacket hanging from the back of the door, trousers and shirt neatly folded, shoes aligned. She admired his child like discipline and he looked calmer than she had ever seen him before. Mel was humbled that she could bring him such peace so quickly; he was clearly at home with her and her heart skipped in knowing that he just might be right for her.

Mel reversed from the room, somehow more secure in knowing Greg was staying with her. She had not felt this way for years, indeed, not since the troubles and end with Sam.

She poured herself a glass of water in the kitchen, catching a sip, before turning the light out in the hall and heading for her bedroom. She whispered good night to Greg as she passed his door and made herself ready for bed.

It had been a long day, and she knew that the following day was going to be full on, but had forgotten the content in the last few hours, truly engaged with Greg, who was now fast asleep in the other room. She almost wanted him to wake and come across the hall, but then she did not want to rush the situation, in part to make sure Greg was ready, but mainly because she wanted to make sure she was ready to take the next steps. Understanding Greg better meant she knew she was, but she would wait all the same.

Her head spun a while as it was enveloped by the down pillow and soft duvet, and not just because she had drunk half a bottle of crisp white wine over dinner. She found herself comforted, excited, and safe. Her eyes closed and she did not stir until morning.

She had thought she had heard the chirp of a mobile phone alarm, forgetting for a split second that Greg was in her apartment, but then happily remembering. It had been years since a man had stayed in that box room and it was the 'dog-house' then, but not this morning. The cloud of the day could just be viewed through the curtains as she stirred, then realising that there were new sounds from the kitchen, as a kettle could be heard boiling and coffee mugs being rescued from the dishwasher. A polite a gentle tap was made at her bedroom door by Greg.

'Hi, come in', discreetly covering the parts not to be seen, well not yet anyway.

'Are you a tea or coffee person?' asked Greg as his thin, lightly haired torso came around the door, faded black boxer shorts just in view.

'Uh...coffee, black, half a sugar please'.

'I'll bring it through and jump in the shower if that's ok'. He smiled, hardly waiting for an agreement as he left her bedroom with purpose.

'Fine...what time is it?', trying to focus, having banished a bedroom clock some years back.

'6.15!'

'Really! You're not one of those really annoying morning people, are you?', she chuckled, gathering her camisole and shorts and knowing that she was the same type now, although that had not always been the case when she was with Sam.

'Sure am!', as he delivered the hot coffee, gave her a confident peck on her pillow-warm, rosy cheek and he left the room, disappearing into the bathroom across the hallway, water pouring soon to be heard and the shower door slamming.

She put on her fawn dressing gown, picked up her coffee mug and wandered into the bathroom. She was not giving him the upper hand in the confidence stakes. Mel felt like a naughty teenager again and loved it.

'And what would Sir like for breakfast before he leaves?', she asked, clearly taking a few moments to admire the view of his watered body through the steamed glass before revealing her presence.

Greg, slightly startled at the surprise, but somehow delighted for the interruption, coughed, 'Wow! Um, any toast…coffee?', covering over parts of his anatomy he felt could be seen, although Mel had already viewed what she needed to see.

Mel laughed. 'You going to let me in there with you sometime?'. She didn't wait for a response, the beaming smile on his face said it all, and she went to the kitchen.

It was clear they both knew the direction they were heading and looked forward to the next evolution.

Time pressed, the rush hour stopped for no one. Greg, now washed, watered and brushing the toast crumbs from his stubbled chin, needed to get to the office. He looked fresh, and far less tired than the previous night. Mel had also slept well, and moved to give Greg a kiss, still in her dressing gown, holding his waist. He reciprocated and they gazed at each other.

'When can I see you again?', they asked almost in unison, both then hesitating then squeezing each other a little bit tighter.

'Soon', she responded softly, 'can I call you later?'.

'Please', not waiting any longer to give her a kiss, this time complete and searching. Mel was ready!

Leaning over the sink, she waved from the kitchen window as his silver car pulled out of the apartment's car park. He flashed his car lights with vigour, dipping his head to beam up to her and then merged into the commuter traffic.

Melissa: Why had he been left on the shelf?

Her phone pinged with a text, simply noting 'Xxxx' from Greg.

Coffee in hand, she found herself standing in her small kitchen, pulling her dressing gown around her neck a little further having noted the chill outside, bemused and excited by what had just happened. Her heart pulsed as she leant against the Formica kitchen top.

She observed a good man in Greg. Kind, attentive, socially awkward, clean, sometimes stubborn, set in his ways, a safe pair of hands, responsible but puerile at the same time, but somehow untouched by the world, almost pristine in his lack of worldly understanding. He was certainly no axe wielding monster. More a Mum's boy grown up and yet still within her grasp. She did not want to change this, but to create a new journey on his canvas that they could both map together. Melissa found this exciting, so much to teach him, to show him, to experiment with him. She knew that for them both there would need to be a transition, and if this went too fast, it may collapse. Transition fatigue if you like, certainly to be avoided. Where would she start?

He had not been called a boring muppet without reason in the past and this was an observed criticism that he was happy to endure. Safe pair of hands? Sure, although he was unlikely to set the world, or any bedroom entertainment, or anything really, alight. But while Mel was asleep, she knew he would be there, ready, 'the Watchman', as his name suggested, and in the morning, she was more likely to be offered a cup of tea than an energetic sex bout that would leave her knackered before her feet had even touched the carpet.

She smiled, she liked this thought, and she knew she could take control of any 'dawn horn' if she wanted it. Was she falling in love with the nerd? Maybe. She was certainly going to keep going to find out.

Greg could be annoying, predictable, with a sense of duty to others that was never returned, all wrapped in a plain wrapper, but he was safe, secure, attentive and, she knew, falling in love with her. Her smile became broader as she dressed, left the flat and headed to work, her daily commute somehow effortless that morning.

Just across the road from the office, she took a crisp plastic £5 note to pay for her Starbucks coffee from her Louis Vuitton purse, a gift to her from Sam on her 40th birthday. A small, old, crinkled photo booth picture fell out at the same time of her and Sam, mucking about and pulling faces. It paused her from her purchase for a second, looking down on it at the floor. Mixed emotions rushed through her mind. She had kept it for years, she even remembered sliding the picture into the purse on her 40th birthday evening, before sinking a bottle of champagne, and then sinking into bed with Sam for a crazy night of sex. It got a bit weird that night, searching boundaries of what they could do, and then going far further. It proved to be the start of the unraveling.

Mel was now in a different place, a surer place with Greg than she had been for a long time. She could let go of the past. A warmth came over her as she reached down and picked the picture up. She did not return it to the purse, but tore it down the middle before putting it in the bin. The release from her hand was a release from her heart. She beamed. Greg was the future, her future she mused, as she crossed the road for her daily grind.

Her grin seemed permanently fixed, and she had a spring in her step, radiating pleasure to her colleagues as she settled at her desk. The paper holder of her coffee mug was warm in her hand. It was already a good day, and no one was going to interfere with that, her head full of Greg's night stop over and what was held in store for the future.

Chapter 9
Maze to amaze

∞∞

A little rusty!

Greg's sex life and experience had been limited, from what he could remember of it. He jokingly thought at one point that he would have 'break seal to open' tattooed around his lower belly in case a woman ever came near him, it had been so long since he had been intimate. Sure, he could still get aroused, but even this seemed to be infrequent of late. He had googled the 'little blue trapezoid' to understand the benefits, and to check that if he did need any 'assistance', that it would not interfere with his blood-pressure pills, prescribed a decade or so back due to the pressures of work.

Mel's previous encounters when love making had not been forgotten. There were a few she could refer to, some good and others...well, you can work it out. Sure, she would rather forget the times when Sam had got a bit weird in the location and requests he had chosen for intercourse, but she could park these and remember the loving times only. And there were many to refer to, pleasing herself that she had got rather good at her technique over time, and this is what she wanted for Greg, to love him well, for him to want her more. Mel had been without a partner for four years now, but was well versed in the opportunities, unlike Greg whose carnal knowledge was at best dated, and he admitted that he was a little rusty when it came to sex, his university days and the limited 'anything' in between.

They both knew that their opportunity was not far away, if they wanted it, and they did. 'I'll be gentle', she assured him, which in itself was enough to arouse him, and she knew this. 'No need' he bluffed, with the look of school boy terror and intrigue written all over his face. Mel gave wry smile, reading his mental predicament well, and she kissed him, her tongue darting across his as their passion rose.

Mel knew where this consuming encounter was heading, and slowed the urges they both shared. She wanted it to be right for them both, to be prepared, to be committed to love. She soon created the opportunity…

Hampton Court Palace

Mel wanted to enjoy a day out with Greg, to be with him, both as a partner, but also as a lover. Greg was clearly nervous about making the first move. She was not sure he ever had, maybe falling into the clutches of a student piss-up on the odd occasion, but to want to love a lover? Hmm, she thought.

Something cultural, historic, with a male interest and not anything to do with cars! 'I know!' she smiled. Hampton Court Palace, historic, good walk round the gardens, Henry VIII and all his wives, which Greg could enjoy and give them something to laugh about, and then she could take him home, give him dinner and put him to bed... 'With me!', she thought. Perfect, a demonic look raising an eyebrow at her cunning. Was she ensnaring him? 'Me? Never! But I'm not going to wait for Greg to make a move. I'll be retired before he finds the right moment and I need to know him now'.

Mel was not shy in hiding her plans from Greg, offering to drive to Godalming to pick him up, so that he did not have to worry about his precious bloody car, one love of his life that he would need to be distracted away from, could have a drink....and more if he wanted it. Anyway, she wanted to see where he lived and possibly to catch a glimpse of his elusive brother Gavin. 'Bring a toothbrush' her closing comment as all was arranged.

Greg was like a schoolboy on the day before a school trip. He even put out an outfit to make himself look more dapper, ensuring that his underwear was not to his usual standard and that his old condoms were in order. They weren't. 'Fuck it', he shouted, then laughed at both the expletive and the planned end use, dashing to the supermarket to be fixated by the choice. Had it been that long since he made a purchase? Greg sighed, knowing it had, reaching forward to grab the standard pack, and the Raspberry Ribbed, his favorite flavour on food at least, having never tried this alternative and not planning to start anytime soon, to indicate that he could add a surprise or two. He felt 30 years younger as he presented his purchases at the counter, the lady behind the counter indifferent to his choices, looking at her watch to see eagerly how close she was to her next coffee break. He allowed himself a confident smile as he left the store, knowing that he may well be 'on a promise!'.

Mel showered and made herself ready for her car journey of about 30 miles to Godalming. Her planning of an outfit had been thought through during the week, dinner was in the fridge and the flat tidied.

Mel wore figure hugging black cropped faded jeans, Converse trainers, with a dark green fitted shirt, and a tan brown Barbour jacket to be ready for her walk around the Palace, whilst looking suitably alluring to Greg, although his desires towards her were becoming self-evident and she shared this desire. A pashmina packed in her handbag just in case the autumn cold arrived, sunglasses against autumn sunshine were the preferred alternative, although she believed her heart would stay warmed by his company.

The journey was unremarkable for a Saturday morning, although she would probably not have noticed as her head swam with Greg in her mind. A radio play spouted from the speakers as she neared his house, something that she had not seen before. 'You have reached your destination' noted the Sat-Nav as she spotted Greg's car, newly washed, on the driveway.

It was 10.30 and Greg invited her in with a light kiss at the door, her perfume beguiling him for a second. 'You look great!' he smiled as he turned and beckoned her into the kitchen, the kettle just bubbling could be heard as she approached. 'Coffee OK?' he questioned, she nodding as he poured and she looked around. Greg, dressed in his faded chinos, dark jacket and trainers seemed to be in a hurry, and was clearly not keen to hang around there. Gavin's presence was in the house, although the brother was nowhere to be seen, Greg noting that he was away on a trip to Austria with friends, although due back soon. The house was modest, clean, but tired, loved by a woman who was now long gone and occupied by two adults who were lost in masculine municipality. Functionality abounded over style and grace, which to some extent was not unanticipated by Mel. Little money had been spent on the house since Greg's parents had passed away, partly due to modest incomes and partly through bickering between brothers about who was paying for what, to a point that conflict was avoided by doing only the bare minimum.

To Greg, it seemed as though they had argued over minutiae all their lives, and just because they were 'mature', well in certain parts of their lives and juvenile in others, why break the habit of a lifetime? There was nothing to break this petty cycle between the brothers, although their sister Rebecca had tried, and the victim of this pettiness was the house, with its threadbare, but hoovered carpet, and worn Formica kitchen tops. He was pragmatic about this, it was not as though they did not share regard for each other, just that it did not seem to work when it came to putting money into the communal pot.

Mel admired the honesty of the home, although she would admit later that she would have had the paint pots in to brighten the place up if it was her domain.

With coffee consumed in the kitchen, coats and Greg's small hold-all were collected together, he locked the house and jumped into Mel's car, still pinking from the trip down to collect him. They chatted all the way to Hampton Court and the Palace, Greg clearly at ease with Mel, and she with him. Mel had done a little research on the website before booking a guided tour, holding hands when the group stopped, taking in the character of each hall, room and corridor they explored. It was a balmy autumn day, with warm sun on their faces as they walked the gardens. The low sun glistened on the Thames as it meandered past the Palace, its grace as magnificent as the building that stood next to it.

The Hampton Court Maze was lots of fun! He admired the fact that it was something that he would not normally do, but the Maze itself was not the draw, it was Mel, being with her, wanting her. He jokingly suggested that at every dead end they explored, they must kiss, 'almost a game of kiss-chase' he laughed, with Mel lunging forward with a smile and planting a big kiss on his lips, adding 'start as we mean to go on', grabbing his hand and leading him into the entrance, almost deliberately finding obvious dead ends in which to kiss. The chill in the air had kept visitor numbers down, and with a few autumn leaves littering the floor, they went deeper into the Maze, their kisses became more intense, lustful, with no one to spy on them. Mel took a selfie of them together and Greg needed to compose himself at one point as his arousal was becoming obvious, and certainly to Mel who was enjoying stimulating him. Neither had any idea how long a trip round the Maze should take, but they had been in there a long time, and enjoyed every second of the additional kiss-chase game they had added to the experience.

The fresh air made them hungry, although what they both wanted was not on the menu of the Terrace Café, as they headed for a late lunch. Desire for each other was overpowering their hunger pangs, and a topped baked potato on the terrace with warm sunshine flitting between the occasional cloud, with a beer and Diet Coke was all that they needed.

A text on his phone chirped. 'You home tonight? G'.

'It's Gavin, clearly just home from Austria', he said, typing into his black-covered mobile, 'No, hope you had a good trip. Gas needs paying'. 'OK' pinged back promptly, Greg almost feeling that his older brother had given him permission to be out all night.

The drive back to Mel's took half an hour. The Saturday traffic was light, as the car lights started to come on and Greg was clearly itching to wash and brush Mel's car up, which was certainly not a priority to her. Mel's flat was warm as they entered and as the evening sky darkened, they prepared dinner, with a bottle of red wine opening early. Mel put the radio and oven on and made ready the table for dinner, Greg helping where he could, learning the locations of various items as he went.

He felt for a moment he was getting in the way of her plans, which seemed carefully choreographed, and to get out of the way, he asked if she minded if he took a shower before dinner. 'Sure! help yourself, you know where it is' she confirmed, adding, 'Want me to scrub your back?', with a cheeky grin.

'Um! Yeah!', he laughed as he left the room and naturally headed to the box room to get undressed before heading to the bathroom and the shower. 'He's not staying in there tonight!', Mel thought as she finished laying the table, then moved his clothes to her room as the water jets could be heard from the bathroom.

She folded his clothes and jacket carefully by the bed, and with everything as she wanted it, she slipped out of her cropped jeans and fitted shirt and joined him. She removed her underwear before holding on to his pale skin as the warm tingling water consumed them both. 'Let's see what your expert car washing skills are really like!', she smiled as they kissed, both knowing that this was what they wanted, needed.

The embrace was passionate, although Greg was a little clumsy in the small cubicle and Mel was ready to help him, her fading tan on her smooth skin contrasting to his lathered pale torso. It was clear that intercourse in the shower would need a bit more practice from them both, and they fled to the bedroom, towels in hand and thrown on the bed covers, neither waiting to towel each other down. Greg grappled for his new condoms, reaching to his newly located jacket, the delay somewhat stifling the moment. Mel was not that concerned, she knew he had not been with someone for years, although Greg seemed determined to use his new purchases, regretfully bemused as he had to concentrate for a second on the selection he had bought. 'WTF!', before picking up the ribbed packet with a knowing smile for Mel's approval, she not caring as she needed him now. Mel helped him pull the protection down to its extent, her nimble, red-tipped fingers showing some experience, he still slightly wet from the shower, before she moved to pull him slowly and deliberately towards her eager body.

Their combined energy was powerful, as Greg entered Mel for the first time, both impatient to feel each other surrounded. His excitement at the thought of this moment had been raging in his body for weeks. This was the first time in a long time that he had been able to truly love another and he countered his breathing to ensure that his explosion was not premature. Mel sank into Greg, the warmth and completeness was breath taking, she too shivering with excitement. Neither was going to last long in this first encounter and Greg did not take very long to reach a point where his desire was overwhelming. For a few seconds his eyes went dewy as his warmth rushed from his body to hers, filling the condom. His pulses of movement quickened and then he flinched above her, Mel holding him tight, juddering with him as she too orgasmed with a man for the first time in years. The amazing sensation for them both was so exciting, discovering something new, but familiar, fun, exhilarating, sensational, that they both wanted to repeat over again. Greg's eye contact was intense as he held Mel, their faces together, he imparting a meaning of love, of care towards her, that she was the one, not just for that moment. His vulnerability was palpable, and she was consumed by love and lust in one go. She kissed him slowly, firmly, assuredly.

They both slumped after their mutual exertion. Greg relaxed and just drifted for a second, his head buried in the pillow savouring the moment. Mel disappeared for a time, returning with the bottle of wine and two large glasses, Greg commenting on her return at 'what a wonderful sight' knowing that he was not just referring to the wine. They sat up in the bed, retrieving for a short time the duvet as they recovered from their tryst. It was clear to Mel when Greg had recovered, as she peeked under the covers to see his erection ready for her.

Mel too needed a little time to recover. She was surprised that years ago, she felt she could go all night with Sam, and sometimes did, ravenous to combine with him again and again. She thought she was fit, but those four long years of life alone had clearly taken their toll on her bedroom energy. 'Need to work on that!' she thought as she guided Greg within her again, Mel on top this time, and started to gently rock with her breasts rubbing softly against his chest as their movement gained synchronicity and then speed. Greg was spell bound as he watched the goddess that was Mel work her magic above him, his arms holding her thighs and gently rocking in time within her. She brushed her hair away as she leant into her kiss with him, their tongues frantic in their search within each other's mouths, Mel watching his eyes for the tell-tale expressions that he may not last much longer. Greg's stamina was extending as they made love, even with a condom on, and she found that her energy levels were being challenged by this up-start rejoining the sex game after so many years. Her skin glistened with perspiration as she found her rhythm in their love making. She was thrilled as her body tingled above him that their love making could be so good so quickly and she climaxed before him, her body shivering as the spasm echoed through her body, and her breathing moved to a moan. Greg had thought for a short time that he was in control of his ejaculation, but Mel's explosion above him was more than enough to send him over the edge and he felt a rushed release from his tightened body, his eyes fixed on Mel and she sat astride him, eyes closed and loving the moment. With both their love needs fulfilled, Mel collapsed onto her side of the bed and pulled the duvet over them both, covering their heads with warmth as she closed her eyes and relaxed in his arms. Both drifted again, more deeply this time and half an hour disappeared before either made a move.

Hunger was on neither of their minds, but the smell of cooking from the kitchen reminded them that dinner was in the oven. Reluctantly, they gathered some clothes together, Mel simply opting for her dressing gown and headed to the kitchen to serve up. It was a rather thrown-together dinner, although neither cared, just chatting and kissing, in between sipping a second bottle of red wine, the first one being emptied after the first love making in the bedroom. They cleared away and went to back to the bedroom, both satisfied with their individual and partner's energetic love-making, although neither were spring chickens any more.

With the duvet and the odd pillow retrieved from the floor, the small double bed seemed a little cramped at first to them both, not normally sleeping with a partner. The excitement of being in each other's arms soon dispelled any desire to head to the edges as their naked bodies rested next to each other. Mel placed a soft kiss on Greg's lips, with a 'see you in the morning', look before closing her eyes and drifting off.

Mel's sleep was deeper than normal, she felt complete, safe in her own home, safer than she normally would with Greg now by her side. She had missed this warmth and welcomed its return. Greg marvelled at Mel as she drifted away, exhausted by his performance that evening, and slightly overwhelmed by what was happening to him, to his life, to his soul. Her make-up was gone and he admired the contours of her beauty, its light blemishes and long eyelashes, her face radiant and serene. He kissed her softly on the forehead and the edges of her lips turned favourably before relaxing into their slumber.

'What had he done to deserve this wonder?' he asked, although sleep gripped him before he could ponder the question further.

The night disappeared with neither leaving each other's side, other than Greg going to relieve himself before sunrise. The morning broke, although both felt that if they could stop the world at that point and get off the treadmill together, they would. An inner peace and excitement cloaked them together beneath the duvet.

Mel felt that Greg had woken, he kissing her shoulder gently, the smell of the lather created in the shower the afternoon before still fragrant, but also the firmness that she felt from him on her bum. Mel turned, her intent clear to Greg, 'Morning' she smiled with a gentle kiss, with Mel climbing on to him, his arousal being promoted further. She didn't want protection this time, she did not want to be protected from Greg. The feeling for them both was far more intense, combined and complete. Greg hesitated for a short second, but as Mel slid over him, the sensation was intoxicating and he put up no resistance. They rolled over, with Greg above her, his palms planted on the mattress, this time the intercourse more involving, slower, melodic and natural to him, almost more committed than before. The feeling was sincere, intense and real, Greg caressing her and kissing her intently, the honour being afforded him more than any other had ever done before. He sweated as the sensation was amazing to him and he needed no words to explain the love that he felt for Mel as their rhythm reached its climax.

As they rested, neither Greg or Mel were in a hurry to rise from the nest they had created together in her bedroom. The sun could be seen to be occasionally tapping on the window through the crack in the part pulled curtains, in between the odd dark cloud.

Mel fixed coffee and this was consumed in bed, chatting as they sipped from their mugs, with both checking their phones to see what was happening in the world. A text from Mel's sister asking if she was coming over this morning, which she declined and a call to the house from her caring but protective mother, who knew there was a 'visitor' to make sure all was OK, but also to make sure it was going well, saying that she could bring him over. It was too early for Greg to face her clan, but the thought of enveloping him in her family was welcome.

Greg offered to wash Mel's car, he had been itching to do this since they had started dating, and Mel tweaked his nipple with her painted nails, Greg letting out a pained grimace, for her to air her objection to the suggestion. She wanted him to be with her, not her car. She added 'now that's a very 'I live here' type of suggestion' to Greg, he apologising, although he knew he did not mean it.

'Can I use the eggs in the fridge door?', he asked, having noted these when helping with the dinner the night before, also checking for butter, knowing that milk was available for teas and coffees.

'Sure…why?', Mel replied, before being interrupted by Greg enthusiastically. 'I make mean scrambled eggs on toast if you're hungry?' he asked, excited by the opportunity to show off. 'Okay', Mel hesitated slightly, knowing that they were not her favourite dish, but happy for Greg to show his culinary skills. 'I'm a rubbish cook, but scrambled eggs. Bellissimo!' leaping from the bed naked and grabbing his boxer shorts and t-shirt with a kiss blown to Mel as he headed for the kitchen, pots and utensils clanging before very long.

She rested in the bed and thought about Greg, their shared passion the night before and a man, who she knew she was falling in love with, rustling up some food in the kitchen. A small tear slid down her face as she felt fulfilled, the first time in four years, and she loved it. Mel wiped the tear away, trying to compose herself because others would follow if she did not. She didn't want to creep Greg out, although she knew that he was not far from her in the emotion stakes, and she loved that as well.

She was lost for a few minutes and interrupted by a 'Ta-Dah!' as the bedroom door opened, and Greg appeared with two plates of steaming scrambled eggs, his only signature dish. It was good…very good and Mel kissed him softly and slowly to thank him, before the plates were placed out of reach and they combined again with each other, their mutual rhythm now beginning to be familiar and in unison.

Greg stayed the Sunday and headed home to Godalming and his brother Gavin in the late afternoon, as the light began to fade, to be ready for work in the morning, but mainly because he had not brought enough clothes to reach over two nights. Greg also somehow did not want to outstay his welcome. He could not be more complete than when he was with Mel and he realised that he was in love.

Mel also felt that she did not want him to go. Not just tonight, back to his home, but really forever. She wanted to start living again, with Greg, together. Was this love? Nothing had been clearer to her!

Chapter 10
What should not be....is?

Mel was finding her ability to love Greg effortless. Had she tried too hard to love someone in the past, when, if she had simply relaxed into the person she had met, it would have simply clicked? Or was that some fantasy drivel reserved for some well-thumbed romantic novel, with its coloured spine fading on some back-room shelf?

Or was it the man, Greg? Had she swiped right quicker with some other geek, would she have found love earlier? It was certainly the man. Greg seemed untouched, new even. With her new-found knowledge that there was a whole sector of men that she, and it appeared most others on the dating scene, willingly ignored by swiping left, should she now look at this untapped oasis of love to see if there were any better Greg types in the dating pool that might suit her well? The thought hesitated and fluttered across her mind for a few seconds and then naturally fell, as she thought of Greg and her heart lifted at his childish charm, willingness to be loved, and his new found knowledge on how to love her in bed. This idea dismissed, it certainly was the man, Greg, who was what she needed. She and Greg should not should not work...at all...but they did, their synergy was palpable! 'I love a nerd' she laughed to herself, 'My nerd!' she said to herself. It was a powerful realisation.

Mel's only concern was that she wanted the buzz that he gave her to last forever. Her comfort with him was complete, but she did not want this to progress over to become a comfy pair of slippers type of relationship, drinking cocoa together in the early evening before going to bed by 9.00 pm. She didn't mind the idea of going to bed early, but only to feel Greg inside her as they loved together. She had noticed that his stamina was lasting even longer, which she very much approved of, and he was clearly enjoying his education.

Greg was bewildered by his 'lost in space' feelings for Mel. He was not sure he had experienced such a varied surge in feelings for another. Some of these wonderful feelings he had never experienced before and he loved it, but was also confused how someone could simply reach into his life and turn it upside down. He ran his fingers through his hair and realised he had not been under the clippers for a couple of weeks. 'Not at all good!', he thought, if he was seeing Mel later. Another sign to him that his attention spans were being distracted, and probably an outward sign to anyone else that he was in fact very much in love. He had understood this, he just needed to adjust to this unfamiliar space.

He drove to a local parade of shops and visited the usual barber that he frequented. It was the sleazy end of masculine, with deeply ingrained testosterone mingling with the hair clippings, aftershave and hair wax. The waiting bench was nearly full and he tucked himself into the remaining slot, grabbing a scruffy car magazine as he sat down. Watching your phone's contents seemed to be the order of the day for the younger victims of the shearers before them, with the older men reading the papers, or starring into space. The wait could be half an hour, but he did not care. Indeed, he did not even notice the time drift by as he found himself comfortably dreaming of Mel and what could be, and was. He was happy and was not listening when he realised that half the shop was staring at him as the barber shouted, 'Who's next?', to get his attention.

He blushed and gathered himself together, keeping his jacket on and taking the faux leather red chair as the clippers sprang into life. It never seemed to matter what you asked for at this barbers, the achieved cut always looked the same, both on him and most of the others he had observed. But it was smart, groomed and tidy and he hoped that Mel would notice his effort. He grinned to himself and drifted again as the tattooed and bearded barber roamed around him with grace, and of course, the occasional nick at the neck line.

With £25 parted from his wallet, he left and entered the dank air of the street, a distinct freshness to the last hour. He refreshed his neck line from clippings and took a selfie, texting it to Mel: 'Trimmed and ready for action!'.

He headed for the car, his phone tinging: 'Oh! Sexy! So, which hair am I going to run my nails through?', Mel texted.

Greg blushed, then smiled, his fingers responding: 'Show you later! Leaving now, be with you soon, XXX'.

Mel put her phone down on the sofa, smiling with a warm glow as to her day ahead with Greg, her newly painted toes glistened with their red sheen as they finished their dry. Toes on the coffee table, she pondered for a moment. He was mysterious in some respects, partly because he had not truly discovered himself before. It was almost as though they were taking his journey together. She had never thought of herself as a 'Tour Guide' before, taking him on a journey through the continent of Greg that remained largely unexplored. She did not have a map, just intuition and there were things to change, sure, things to adjust, but in all nothing of significance, but with love and time the match would be, well, perfect. She tingled at the thought that love could be found again, could be shared, could be caressed, and satisfied physically together. She had not realised how much she had missed sex, and Greg was getting better at that part, of course with Mel's adept wisdom between the sheets.

Where would she take the next stage of her tour? She knew when...this afternoon!

Not so secret retail therapy

It was to some extent a test of Greg to take him shopping in the town. She had an inkling that it was not going to be in his 'Top 10' of activities, as was the case for many men, but she knew that this was just part of the jigsaw that she needed to put together in her hearts file, labelled Greg.

The shopping trip to the High Street was not as inspiring as the designers would have wanted you to experience. The choices were vast across the various shops, Mel clearly having great knowledge of what shop was where and what bargains could be sought, if you knew what you were looking for. Greg was trying very hard to engage with a topic he knew little about, but was more than happy just to be with Mel on this Saturday afternoon. He had driven over that morning and with coffees consumed, drove into town to experience retail therapy Mel style.

Having the opportunity to sit in shops, along with many uninterested husbands on tired-looking sofas with the remnants of this week's paper filled him with horror. However, Mel would come out of the changing booth to give him a twirl and he relished the opportunity to openly admire her curves, ones that he had only recently had the opportunity to get to know. Indeed, any other man doing the same got a scowl from him, with a not so polite cough to say, 'she's mine!'. He had never felt protective before in such a way, and he loved it. She laughed and went back into the booth to change back into her favorite jeans that she now fitted and re-complimented her new figure recovered from the past, black boots edged in gold, a must from a recent flash sale, and her fitted jumper.

With selected purchases made, Greg made jesting 'hee-haw' noises as they walked down the High Street carrying the bags, as if he were her donkey. She slapped him lightly to stop him, but he continued with sporadic laughing.

'Finished yet?', she smiled.

'Maybe!', he grinned.

'I'll make you smile!' Mel confirmed, reaching a high-end lingerie shop at the bottom of the road, indicating her intent to finish her shopping there. She had not originally planned to, but if Greg was going to be playful, so was she, just in a different way later. She knew he would be uncomfortable, and kissed him at the entrance, darting her tongue into his mouth for a second, eyes open and then giving him a slow wink. Any concerns evaporated from Greg's mind instantly.

Mel headed straight for the entrance, knowing she would receive little resistance from Greg, his joke animal noises silenced in an instant at what lay ahead. He was not disappointed and could not help but feel that some of the attire was inspired as his eyes fixed on a gravity defying creation that instantly distracted him.

Mel was keen to treat Greg to some of the situations he had not enjoyed before, as far as she knew. The shop was large and packed. There was nothing secret about anything, the irony in the name of the shop made him smile. 'Blue or maybe silver, what do you think?', Mel asked, displaying two sets of lingerie against her body, her smooth red fingernails contrasting with both and trying her best to add on some barely legal, in public anyway, burlesque style movements. A warm but carnal smile crossed his face, his eyes focused like an angelic serpent, as he watched her subtle gyrations as he considered the choice being offered. 'Mmmm', more from a 'what's not to like with any of the garments on view', rather than a choices-choices perspective. 'Both of them?', was his final reaction. She knew what he was thinking, and pleased with it! 'Work round these can you?' not waiting for a response before selecting her size in both colours, placing them in her basket and heading immediately towards the Basque section, Greg dutifully and happily following.

He observed younger generations shopping together, wondering why this never happened when he was a student, older men looking bored glued to their phones, assistants ensuring you had everything you needed, all mixed with loud music and videos of scantily clad models on catwalks. He could think of worse ways to be parted from his cash, if indeed he was paying. He was not going to argue!

The return to the car and home was not particularly rushed, although as soon as the door closed the trying on (and off) of the new purchases was almost immediate. Mel stripped and picked the first available matching pair, blue selected first, before presenting them to Greg, perched eagerly on the bed side, legs wide to bring her closer to him. 'So, what do you think?'. Greg's Cheshire Cat grin and 'boy in sweetie shop' eyes did not really require an answer. 'Well let's see! Kiss-chase?' he whispered, reminded of the time in the Maze, as his arms came around to embrace her waist, kissing her stomach softly, Mel leaning in to accept, before he moved gently up to un-cup her breast from its new soft lacy embrace to accept this willingly into his searching mouth.

Greg was warm to this embrace. He had never thought of himself as a tactile sort, but wanted nothing more at that point, or any of the other times they had made love together. To be loved, to love was more than he could contain and their heightened love making was now more assured, rather than the first few times, which were more frantic in their original lust. Slower, tender, but somehow deeper in its intensity, its meaning, its honesty and totality. 'I love you' he whispers as he moves deeply within her, needing to tell Mel, although this has been clear for some time. She holds him tighter to acknowledge his desire without comment as her body heightens the rhythm of their joining, her heart racing with desire. Greg feels a tear on his cheek from her and looks into her eyes, the joy on her face is complete and Mel kisses him firmly, her tongue welcoming his to ensure that he knows she loves him too.

'I love him!

Her stride into the office exuded confidence, nearly verging on arrogance, even nonchalance, and all her colleagues knew that she was the cat that had got the cream. The prying questions from her friends were becoming more pressing as the days moved by, her attitude lifted, less serious, but somehow more focused. The unusually frequent texting to her phone from Greg was a give-away and it didn't take them long to work out that there was finally a man in her life who really meant something to her. Delighted for Mel, the offers of social gatherings, with new man in tow came often. She resisted, she wanted to savour the time with Greg alone for as long as she could.

Mel felt that as she got older she needed to absorb more of, well, everything. Her desire to embrace her surrounds, their sights, sounds, wonder, wherever they were grew every year. Partly driven by fear, she had seen her parents grow old and seen their sensory perception diminish. She wanted to almost compensate by growing her personal repertoire so that when she came of an age when she too saw deterioration, she could have more personal experiences to keep her mind lively, engaged and ultimately interested, which had been the most devious ailment of her parent's mutual ageing.

Every possible opportunity to be together was taken, with dates, staying over at Mel's and occasionally at Greg's, as long as there was no risk of Gavin interfering, although Mel was introduced to him at one stage. Gavin seemed as she would have expected, and slightly dismissive of Greg as he packed his car for a trip to Devon with friends. He would also grow up one day, maybe just not yet, Mel thought.

With Halloween complete, and thoughts turning to Christmas, Mel arranged a Sunday lunch at a pub, where by coincidence, although clearly fully orchestrated, all of her family were there. Greg gave her a knowing look as he was introduced to the clan, she being concerned that he might have wound himself up if it had not just happened 'by chance'. He chastised her as they made love that evening at her home and she took extra time to kiss him all over, whispering 'sorry' in-between each kiss, not that she was at all and he knew it.

Greg even hit it off with Mel's Dad, who could be grumpy when forced into a family situation. He and Greg looked as bewildered as each other at one point and with beers placed in front of them both, the afternoon disappeared. Another hurdle complete, the immediately approving WhatsApp family group messages from her sisters and mother pinging on her phone were nothing other than approving.

Mel was complete as they left the pub and made their way home to her flat, taking a short walk to Mel's car, holding hands as they went, and deliberately nudging each other hard, with smiles and laughs, partly in knowing they were to be and what was to come when they got home together.

'Greg?' she questioned as they rested in her bed, Greg staring straight at her hazel eyes with a warm complete glow, resting on his pillow from his exhaustion of making love to Mel.

'Come and live with me?', she asked.

Greg, his exhaustion tagged to one side at the suggestion. 'I love you, but'…he hesitated a moment, his eyes welling with tears, Mel terrified immediately that she had mis-read the love and joy that they were sharing.

Greg was softly shaking, tears now clear to be seen as he slipped calmly and slowly from their bed, but only to go on one knee facing her naked, his breathing heavy and focused, 'Maybe we could marry?' he asked softly with a smile, with a searching look into her eyes.

Her fear disappeared as his proposal made her beam, letting out a small cry as she nodded, 'Yes! Yes!, their lips meeting, tears now freely rolling down her cheeks with sheer joy, Mel soon joining him. 'Thank you!' she whispered, as they closed their eyes and held each other tight.

This geek, this Greg was released and he loved it.

Pick one at random

Epilogue

Explaining the many ribbons of love is never truly possible and the way they weave through a life can also be unexplained in many instances. Some will try. When one strand of love is possibly understood, it opens many more directions to explore and the evolution never really ends. The journey itself is never a straight path, and there are no rules in understanding why the lives of two people that you might not imagine being together flow with such consuming grace.

The real person that an individual may be might also be a stranger to that soul, just waiting for someone to love them and to come and unlock their inner being to find themselves. The transition can be painful, fun, heart-rending, unexpected and welcome. The time taken to reach a desire to want to embrace this inner change can happen quickly or take years. We all know people whose journey seems to be an endless road, with them ending before they reach love.

Once there, how do you reach out to others to say you are ready? For some it is natural, and for others, as we have read, the path of love may be twisting, tiresome and hard. Love rarely arrives on your doorstep with a smile and a 'Fancy a coffee, love, relationship?' approach. It evolves, you just have to open your eyes, to search for what is possible, and the excitement can begin!

Why stop at finding love? Search your world for all the possibilities!

Greg has been rescued by Mel and this story has a happy ending. This geek, nerd, call him what you will, had become a man and he will be forever grateful to Mel for sharing her journey with him.

The conclusion to the story is not of one woman and one man discovering that under the faded veneer of averageness there is a good person to be enjoyed underneath. It is that there are tens of thousands of single 'Greg' types, both male and female, out there that need rescuing, largely from themselves.

These are good, if not great, people, who do not know how to express themselves, to share themselves, to make the first move. They just need to be reached, contacted and returned to the fold of humanity that some of them left years ago, residing on the planet that they now live on. They may not be looking for love, they may not know how to, but neither have they been asked, and many, many thousands would like to be across our globe. You do not have to look far, don't be shy.

Sure, there are those who like to be alone, who were made to be alone and they are to be respected, for their self confidence in their objectives, but that is not for all.

They are not left on the shelf, it's almost as if they did not know a shelf existed. Each has their own unique, individual story as to why, and by the time there is this surprise discovery in their life, asking about how to get on and off the perch is all a bit too embarrassing to ask about. And the alternative, loneliness is a parasitic, even demanding friend for anyone to share their lives with on a long term basis, but many do. To share their lives is their objective and how wonderful is that?

The era they grew up in, that Greg grew up in, was not of this age. They had no coaching in life skills, political correctness, in social interaction, you either got it or you didn't and damn the consequences. Political correctness has buried their SOS messages even deeper, for fear of offending any preferences, shallow or not, and for some this is the final nail in the coffin of ever finding love. Their social isolation is complete.

Rebecca

'I have cried with joy at the news of Greg moving in with Mel and getting engaged. She is fabulous, caring, worldly wise with so much positive energy, all the things that Greg has needed adding to his life. He is a good, caring man, misunderstood and how we managed to let him go so geeky I will never know; however he is a loveable geek, he always was, he just needed to be uncovered. I think Mel will achieve this. I am so pleased for them and I know that Mum would be as well. One down, now for Gavin!'.

'Now, time to go shopping for a dress and a hat!'.

Gavin

'Yeah! He's going, I finally get my own personal space! I'm pleased for him, he's changed, for the better, but he needed to. Shit! I need to do something about me now!'

Gabby

'Wow! Uncle Greg is soooo cool now! Mel is great fun and he seems like a different man! Awesome! Hopefully Mel will throw that awful jacket of his away as soon as she can!'.

'Mum, do I get to be a bridesmaid and can I have a new dress?'.

Greg

'Where to start? Never to stop! My journey to Mel has been long and hazardous. I nearly lost myself in the labyrinth of my mind and it was only when Mel touched my soul that I knew what I was looking for. The path to safety, in her arms, was then clear and the burden of the first 49 and a half years seems lifted'.

'I still don't know what made her swipe right. It might have just been fate, or something like that, but I thank her for her love, her care, her energy, her sharing and her being. Welcome to Chapter Two of my life, I can't wait to write it with Mel as my wife'.

Mel

'The beauty of someone to love is not pinned to their shoulder to read. You have to look deeper to understand what makes them tick, makes them exist and it took a second chance meeting to read Greg properly. He is lovely. I may have to 'adjust' him a bit, but he is perfect, and I love him. I said it, I love him and I know he loves me. I'm welling up now, I need a hug...Greg!'.

'Is Greg still a nerd? Sure thing, but he's my nerd now!'.

...and you?

These wonderful people are not hard to find, they are all around us, but because they do not dazzle, or sometimes raise their hand, they blend into and become part of the furniture that many do not see, day to day, or week to week.

See if you can spot them soon, don't swipe left, be like Mel...go and rescue one.

About the Author

Marion Crick

Marion has now been writing for quite a few years and hopefully you have caught up with her first few books, the Lovedon series as an example. If you have already read these, don't worry; Marion still thinks there is another twist in this tale and has penned a few thoughts as she wrote this latest book.

In terms of her background, the close knit community she shared with her parents and sibling were kind to her as she grew up, before finally taking the leap to administration duties in London when her experience of the daily commuter grind began. The after-work social scene was worth the hassle, let alone the elevated salary that came with it, enjoying many adventures in love before settling down, although there was not to be a 'happy ever after' just yet.

Separation, divorce, grieving and re-engagement into the social scene and into dating have all been part of the kaleidoscope she calls her life. This second round of coupling reminded her a little of those first few years in London, when she began to discover herself and her physical and emotional needs.

Can you reach middle age? Is there such a thing these days, and if so, how can you define this? Marion's middle age has not hampered her exploration of re-ignited love, sex and real companionship. Marion always maintained a diary, on and off. She extended this to a daily update after her initial separation, partly of the day's events, good and bad, but also of her inner feelings and the reaction of her friends and family as they evolved, and as her new love and desire exploded.

Marion's diaries have many other revelations within them and *Lovedon* is only part of her story and the stories yet to be written.